RIVER RAMPAGE

BOOK

The Sam Cooper Adventure Series

MAX ELLIOT ANDERSON

RIVER RAMPAGE
The Sam Cooper Adventure Series - Volume 3
Published by Port Yonder Press LLC
Shellsburg, Iowa
www.PortYonderPress.com

ISBN 9781935600152

Edited by Chila Woychik
Copyedited by Heidi Kortman

Illustrations by Anna O'Brien
Book design by behindthegift.com
A SharksFinn Book: an imprint of Port Yonder Press

First edition

Printed in U.S.A.

RIVER RAMPAGE

PROLOGUE

When he first moved to Florida, Sam Cooper thought that his summer vacations would be no different than those in all the other places he had lived before. He'd get out of school, go home, and wait through another boring summer till it was time to go back to school again in the fall. Well, so far it hadn't turned out that way.

He'd met his new best friend, Tony Dodds. Tony's father owned Dodds' marina where Sam took a scuba diving class. You can read all about that in the book, *Lost Island Smugglers*.

He'd also met Tyler Peterson who was practically connected to Tony at the hip, they were such good pals. Like Sam, Tony loved adventure. But he was also a bit of a risk-taker. He didn't break the law or anything. Tony simply enjoyed a challenge.

Tyler was known as a goof-off kinda guy who was always ready with something to say. He acted different when he was away from his mother, and he was easily frightened. Whenever that happened, his eyes blinked real fast. Sometimes it also made his head jerk. Sam hoped that Tyler's parents could continue working out how to become a real family again after their divorce.

Sam nearly drowned with his two friends in the biggest storm to ever hit their area, and then they were stranded on Lost Island. Sure, they were finally rescued, but not before exposing an international smuggling ring which used high-powered speedboats. Okay, that might have been enough adventure for most guys, but then, Sam Cooper wasn't like most guys. He loved all kinds of adventure, from the little things like fixing up an old boat with a crusty sea captain (you can read about that in *Captain Jack's Treasure*), to the really big stuff like those smugglers and speedboats.

His dad joked that Sam had a little MacGyver blood flowing through his veins. Remember MacGyver? He was that TV character who got into, and out of, all sorts of cool adventures by being really, really creative. Sam's father even bought him the whole DVD boxed set!

After he and his friends made it through the trouble on Lost Island, they should have been able to take it easy for the rest of the summer. But those who think that, don't know Sam Cooper. That's probably why he suggested to his friends that they get involved in fixing up the old boat for Captain Jack. Of course, at the time, he thought the captain was going to search for sunken treasure. But that's another story, one you can find out about in *Captain Jack's Treasure*. And what a story it is!

Lost Island Smugglers. *Captain Jack's Treasure*. Wasn't that enough adventure for a whole summer, or even a lifetime? Nope! Sam Tony and Tyler were just getting started! Their next adventure begins with a phone call.

RIVER RAMPAGE

TABLE OF CONTENTS

CHAPTER 1

TONY'S BIG PHONE CALL

Sam was outside catching up on yard work when he heard his phone ring in the distance. He hoped it would be Tony because he remembered what Tyler said when they first met. *"Just remember, if you get a call from Tony, it'll be for something big."* Sam dropped his rake and dashed toward the back door of his house as if he were in the race of his life.

Tony had told Sam that he went on buying trips with his dad. That thought went through Sam's mind because it meant that he might get to visit lots of interesting places he'd never see otherwise. Tony'd also reminded him that if he didn't answer his phone, he'd just call the next person on his list.

Tyler warned him more than once, "These trips could come at any time; winter, summer, spring, or fall."

From what Sam had already heard, Tony never failed to return from one of his adventures without some of the wildest stories anyone told. In fact, kids could hardly wait for school to start in the fall, just so they could hear where Tony had been and what he'd done.

So, at three o'clock in the afternoon on the second Saturday of the second month of summer vacation, Sam yanked the door open, skidded around a kitchen counter, made a final mad dash toward the call he hoped would change everything, and grabbed for the phone after only four rings.

Sam had to hide the fact that he was short of breath, and his heart pounded so hard, it nearly leaped right out of his chest. "Hello," he said in the dullest tone of voice, which reflected exactly how he felt at that very moment. He walked toward the den.

"Who died?" his friend asked.

Sam's heart sank when he heard it wasn't Tony on the other end. "Not funny, Tyler."

"Huh?"

"My dad hasn't been out of the hospital very long, remember?"

"Oh yeah, sorry."

Sam sprawled out in a recliner. "It's just that I'm about to go out of my mind, I'm so bored. You doing anything interesting for the rest of the summer?"

"Am I doing anything interesting? Are you kidding? I just had a call from Tony and guess what?"

"I give up. What?"

"He invited me to go on the most amazing trip I've ever

heard of."

"You? How come you?"

"'Cause we're best friends, I guess."

Sam stood up and began waving his arm in the air and pacing around the room. "Well, what about me? I thought I was best friends with you guys, too."

"You are."

"Then?"

"You'll have to talk to Tony about that, but let me tell you where I'm going."

Sam sighed as he slumped back into the chair. "I can't wait."

"It's a wild rafting trip on the Colorado River."

"*You* lucky."

"I know, I know. We get to go for a whole week, camp on the riverbank, eat out under the sky. It's gonna be great."

"As great as camping out on Lost Island?" Sam asked.

"You know what I mean."

"Wait a minute," Sam interrupted, "you said we, didn't you?"

"Sure. You get ta go, too. In fact, he's probably trying to call you right now. If he doesn't get through, I'll bet he hangs up and calls somebody else."

Sam turned the phone off and slammed it down on a pile of his mother's magazines. As soon as he did that, it rang again.

He grabbed it and pushed talk. "Look, you idiot. If you don't stop calling me I'm gonna—"

"Gonna what? And hey, I can always call someone else who *wants* to talk to me."

"Tony?"

"Yeah, and I don't especially like being called an idiot. Not when I'm about to offer you the trip of a lifetime."

"Lifetime? I'm only twelve. And because of you, I've lived a couple of cat's lives already this summer."

"And?" Tony said.

"Don't tell me it never gets any better."

"Oh, it's about to. That is, if your parents will let you."

"Let me what?"

"You remember me talking about my Uncle Harlan? He lives out west."

Sam shifted in his chair. "I remember you saying something about him before, why?"

"Why? *Why*? Well, for the last three years he's been leading groups of people on these wild Colorado River adventures and guess what?"

"You and Tyler are going."

Tony raised his voice. "How did you know that?"

"He just called me."

"He did? So that's why your line was busy. Well, can you go?"

"I'll have to wait till my parents get home so I can ask. Can I call you later?"

"Sure."

"How soon are you...I mean...*we* going?"

"The rafts leave first thing Thursday. I'll email you a list of all the junk you need to bring. Watch for it in about five minutes."

"Great. I'll call you tonight."

"Boom."

Sam liked the way Tony ended his calls. He went to the computer and opened his email. Then he waited for Tony's message to pop up. When it did, Sam saw that it was a forward of an email from Tony's Uncle Harlan.

"Tony," the email began. "Can't wait to see your Florida bones out here in the wild, wooly, wilderness. This will be more fun than the time we went hang gliding a couple of years ago."

Sam smiled. *That's our Tony.*

"Here's a list of things you need to bring. We take care of all the food because if you're outta food out here, you're outta luck."

That line sent a shiver down Sam's back. He wasn't overweight by any means, but he liked to eat at least three times a day with snacks in between. The thought of being totally out of food worried him a little. He continued reading on to see that he'd need a sleeping bag, swimming trunks, a few changes of clothes, plastic bags to keep everything dry, and lots of other items on a very long list.

Sam's mother was still shopping and his father had started back to work since his heart scare. He wouldn't be home for another two hours. Sam could hardly wait to find out if it would be okay to go.

When his mother returned home at around four-thirty, and he met her at the garage door, he noticed her surprised look.

"I'm shocked," she said. "Usually I have to threaten you

before you help me with the groceries."

He bolted toward the car. "I know, but I have something very important to talk to you about."

"And here I thought you'd made a change this summer to be more helpful around the house," she called back to him.

After he'd dragged all the bags of groceries and other things she'd bought into the kitchen, Sam found his mother putting things away on the shelves in the pantry.

"Mom, I have something to ask you."

"Just let me finish with these and start dinner first."

A sense of panic overtook him, and he could feel his chest tighten. "But it could be the most important question of my entire life." He began rapidly handing her cans and jars faster than she could grab them. "Here. This should help you get done faster."

His mother turned around and put her hands on her hips. "What's gotten into you anyway, Samuel Clement?"

"Nothing," he said, as he continued trying to hand more boxes, bags, cans, jars, and plastic containers to her.

She slightly shook her head. "Well, whatever it is, I like the change. It'll be nice having some extra help around here while you're home the rest of this summer."

Sam quit what he was doing. "That's just it. I have a chance to go away."

His mother stopped restocking the pantry shelves, turned around again, and looked at him. "What exactly are you talking about?"

"You know how I'm always coming home and telling you

and Dad about the great trips Tony gets to take?"

She squinted back at him and slowly nodded. "Some of those stories were pretty frightening. And it's because of Tony you've already been in trouble this summer."

"I know, but this is different."

"How different?"

"He has this uncle. His name's Harlan and he lives out west someplace. The guy takes people on river rafting trips out there."

His mother turned around again and began arranging her shelves. "Well, I hope Tony has a great time so he can come home and tell you *all* about it."

"You don't understand. This year he wants me and Tyler to go with."

"He *what*?" she asked, as a can of soup dropped to the floor.

Sam rushed to pick it up for her. "Tony called me while you were gone. His uncle invited us to come out with Tony and take a trip down the river with the next group."

His mother slowly folded her arms and said, "I'm not so sure about this. Isn't it dangerous?"

"Dad's supposed to call Mr. Dodds and ask all about it. I already have a list from Tony's uncle and everything." He folded his hands together and raised them up to his face. "Oh...please say I can go."

His mother walked across to the other side of the kitchen, leaned forward, put her hands on the counter, and then turned toward Sam again. "We'll have to talk to Dad when he gets home."

Sam's face brightened. He could hardly hide his smile. "You mean you're not saying no?"

She shook her head. "Not yet. I just want to be sure you'll be safe."

Sam raced toward his mother and threw his arms around her. "Oh thank you, Mom. Thanks a lot."

"No one's said you're going yet."

"I know," he said, as he ran toward the door leading to the garage. "And no one said I'm not either."

When Sam reached the garage, he climbed the ladder up toward rafters where he began searching for some of the things on his list. A few minutes later he heard the garage door opening down where he was beginning to make a pile. He stopped, looked down from the rafters, and shouted, "Dad's home!"

In a flash of speed, he met his father before he could even open the car door. "Hi, Dad. How was your day?"

His father gave him an odd look. "You've never asked me that question before in your whole life."

He took his father by the arm. "You want me to get the paper? Your chair is right this way, just waiting for your tired bones to sink down in it so you can take a quick nap before supper."

Sam led him toward the den. "Since when are you so interested in my comfort?" he asked, as Sam pulled him by the arm.

"Hey, like they say. If the dad ain't happy, ain't nobody happy."

"It's the momma…not the dad."

"It is? Oh, yeah."

His father continued looking at him.

"What's the Momma?" Sam's mother asked, as she walked into the room.

"Something has happened to our son and they left this new boy in his place," Sam's father said. Then he looked to Sam. "Okay. What is it this time? Tickets to a ballgame? A new bike? What?"

"It's much bigger than any of those," his mother said.

His father moved over, eased into his chair, and sighed. "All right. Suppose you tell me the whole story."

"You tell him, Mom."

She smiled. "Sam has a chance to go on a river rafting trip with Tony and Tyler."

Sam's father sat up a little straighter in his chair. "A what?"

"A river trip, Dad. Can I go?"

"We don't have any rivers like that around here."

"Colorado, Dad. The river's the Colorado."

"Those trips can be very dangerous. I'd need to go with you, but my vacation doesn't start until August."

Sam's mother laughed. "You weren't invited, dear."

"That's right, Dad. Just me, Tyler, and Tony."

"I don't think I want to turn you over to a bunch of people I don't know, on a trip I know nothing about. When were you planning to go?"

"Next week."

"*Next* week?" He shook his head. "Out of the question."

"But why?"

"It's just too soon. We need to look into the outfit that's taking the trip and do some background checking."

"But..."

Then Sam's mother took a folded paper out of her pocket. "I read the email Sam printed out. It looks pretty good to me. And it's Tony's uncle who will be guiding the group."

Sam could hardly believe he heard those words coming out of his mother's mouth. She was usually the one to think the worst and say so first. It gave him a little more courage to push ahead.

"What do we know about this uncle?" his father asked.

Without thinking Sam answered, "He took Tony hang gliding a couple years...uh oh. I shoulda left that part out."

"They went *hang* gliding?" his father asked.

"You remember. I told you about it. And Tony survived that trip okay."

"Your mother and I will have to discuss this after dinner."

"Ohhh," Sam groaned. "I don't think I can eat till I know."

"That's up to you. But you'll still have to wait. And I want to call Tony's parents, too."

"Oh. I forgot to tell you. They wanted to talk to you anyway."

Sam did his best to eat a little food at supper, but his mashed potatoes reminded him of white-capped river rapids and his pork chop looked exactly like one of the rafts. So he stuck his fork in it and started driving it around over the mound of potatoes on his plate.

Less than a minute later, his mother asked, "What in the

world are you doing?"

Sam looked down at his plate. He knew his face must be turning red because he suddenly felt like the furnace had just come on, on one of the hottest days in Florida. He looked back up and smiled. "Sorry. I was thinking about something."

His father laughed. "Never would have guessed." He winked. "Besides, I thought you were too old to play with your food anymore." Sam shot back a half-hearted smile.

After dinner, his father read the emails. He went on the Internet and looked at the river-rafting site. It took over an hour and a half. Then he called Tony's father.

Sam heard him talking in the den.

"Yes, Mr. Dodds. It sounds like a great opportunity. How much will it cost?"

Sam's heart started pounding.

"Is that right? And how many adults will be on the trip?"

Suddenly Sam could hardly swallow.

"That sounds good. Well then. I'll have Sam call Tony and set everything up. Thank you for the information. You, too. Goodbye."

Sam let out such a loud yell, it made his father jump and drop the phone.

"Yahoo! I get-ta-go-rafting, I get-ta-go-rafting, I get-ta-go-rafting," he said, as he ran around in a figure eight on the den carpet.

"It still sounds dangerous to me," his father said.

"Well," his mother added, "we're always saying we want

Sam to try new things. And we don't have the extra money right now to give him a chance like this. With all the experienced people who will be on the trip, and no cost, I don't see what could go wrong."

Sam thought that somehow he had been temporarily transported into a different family because this did *not* sound like his mother talking. He almost started looking around for TV cameras to see if he'd stumbled onto some kind of reality show where they'd given him different parents. Then he smiled at her and said, "Thanks, Mom. You're the best."

His father gave him a stern stare.

"Oh…and you're the best, too, Dad."

His father's frown turned to a slight smile. "Just make sure you come back safe."

Sam ran toward his room to call Tony. He yelled back over his shoulder. "Nothing's gonna happen to me out there. I'm sure of it."

CHAPTER 2

RAFTING'S REAL DANGERS

Sam called his friends and within ten minutes they walked into his garage.

"Where are you?" Tony called out.

"Up in the rafters," Sam answered.

Tyler looked up. "Is that supposed to be a joke?" Tyler asked.

"Whadaya mean?" Sam asked, popping his head through the hole and looking down at him.

"Rafters?"

Sam smiled back. "I get it." He climbed down and they

began looking over the camping pile he'd already started in the middle of the floor.

"When we moved here, my dad crammed a bunch of stuff up there he thought we'd never need to see again."

"Shows you what parents know," Tyler said.

"I can't believe your parents let both you guys go," Tony said. His face changed to a big smile. "They must not have read about the rattlesnakes, bees, and dangerous rapids."

"Shhh," Sam cautioned. "You trying to get me kicked off this trip before we even leave the driveway?"

"My mom didn't ask too many questions," Tyler said. "She's just glad to get me out of the house for a few days. I think I was already getting on her nerves."

Sam looked up. "How do you know that?"

"'Cause my dad brought her a stack of camp brochures on his last visit. She was looking for any place that would still take me for the rest of the summer. One of them was from Yugoslavia, I think."

"You're kidding, right?" Tony said.

"About Yugoslavia? Yes. But she was getting desperate."

"Well, I think we found a much better place to go than Yugoslavia," Sam said. "Even if it's for only a week. Did you guys bring your copies of the list?"

Each boy took out the information. They sat on a stack of softener salt bags to go over everything.

"Yup," Tyler said as he stroked his chin. "The first thing I'm gonna pack is my shaving kit."

Tony laughed. “I read the list already and crossed off the things we don’t have to bring.”

“Like what?” Tyler asked.

“None of us is on any medication so we don’t need that. And I’m not bringing my digital camera.”

“But I do want my binoculars,” Sam said.

Tony nodded. “Those would be great.”

Then Tyler crossed something off his list.

“What was that one?” Tony asked.

“Well, I decided a long time ago that I was never wearing anything called a fanny pack. Just the sound of it makes me want to…”

“Never mind,” Sam broke in. “My dad has three old army duffel bags. I see here that they say to bring those and to line them inside with plastic bags.”

“That’s to keep everything dry,” Tony said.

“How they gonna get wet?” Tyler asked.

Tony turned to him. “You’re kidding, aren’t you?”

“No, I’m not.”

Sam looked to Tyler. “Have you ever seen one of those TV shows where a rubber raft goes streaking down the river, through a canyon? The people look like they’re about to be swallowed up by a giant wave on the river.”

Tony rubbed his hands together. “Yeah, and there’s all those boulders on the sides just waitin’ to smash the boat. It’ll be the best roller coaster you’ve ever been on.”

Tyler held up his hands. “I hate roller coasters. And besides,

I thought this was just supposed to be a lazy raft trip where we drift along in the calm water and dangle our feet over the side all day long."

"No, you didn't," Tony said.

He nodded and sat up a little straighter. "Yes, I did. If my mother knew we could be killed…wait a minute. They *were* trying to get rid of me."

"Yeah, but for the summer. Not for the rest of your life," Sam said. "And I think Tony's uncle will take good care of us. He's been guiding these trips for three years."

"Hey, I like my uncle and everything," Tony said, "but you guys gotta know something. He's crazier than I am."

"Nobody could be that crazy," Tyler said.

"Wait till you meet him then."

Sam stood up and looked at the pile on the floor. "We still need to finish our lists. I know we'll have to buy some more stuff."

"Like what?" Tyler asked.

"Let's see. I don't have a poncho or a cord to hold sunglasses around my neck, an air mattress, or a fishing license."

Tony looked at the list. "Says here that's optional."

"Good," Tyler said. "I hate fishing anyway, remember?"

"That's all we need is for you to be fishing off a rubber raft."

"Why?"

"Because, with the way you fish, you'd probably get your hook stuck in the raft and flatten the thing."

Sam looked up from his list. "I need a new bug spray and

some sunscreen." He turned to Tony. "And since you don't wanna bring your good one, we should each buy a waterproof disposable camera."

"Looks like our moms'll be hittin' the stores before we leave," Tony said.

Sam looked back at his list. "If anyone has two of something, make sure to let the others know so we can borrow it."

Tyler shook his head. "Not me."

"Why not?"

"No way I'm sharing my toothbrush, comb, or underwear with you guys."

Sam looked at him and sighed. "Not stuff like that. I mean another sleeping bag or air mattress."

"Oh."

Sam handed the extra duffel bags to Tony and Tyler. "Well, then. You guys go on home and see what else you have. I'm gonna start packing."

"I can hardly wait," Tony said.

Tyler looked at his friends. "Me, too…I think."

After his friends had gone, Sam began sorting out his camping gear. He made several piles depending on what he thought he'd never need, up to the items he expected to need right away. The things he didn't need went to the bottom of the duffel bag first. That's because an army bag has only one big opening at the top. In order to reach something at the bottom of the bag, everything has to come out again.

Later that evening, Sam sprawled out on the couch and

started flipping with the remote. He ran through the usual shows until he came to one about whitewater rafting. In this program he watched large rubber rafts rise up high on the water one moment, and seconds later they disappeared as if the river had swallowed them whole. He sat up and gulped as he began to picture himself in one of those rafts. A cold chill went right through him when he thought about the dangerous trip he was about to take. As he continued to watch the program, the people in the raft looked so helpless against the river's fury. Each time the raft dipped out of sight and then shot back up like a rocket, several people on the raft screamed. That put goose bumps all over his arms.

Better not let my parents see this, he thought. So he quickly changed to a baseball game. But he couldn't stop thinking about those poor people on the raft. After only a few minutes, he flipped back to the river show. Something must have happened because several people sat on the riverbank. They were completely soaked and now their raft was only a flat hunk of black rubber. The next shot he saw was of all their belongings bobbing up and down as they raced away in the raging rapids. Some of the women were crying.

That could be us out there. The thought sent a sudden shudder through his entire body. It also made him wonder if this river adventure was such a good idea after all. But it was too late now. He didn't want to look like a chicken by backing out at the last minute. And he didn't want people to think he was afraid like Tyler, even though he was…a little. He also didn't want to back out of it because finding something fun to do that both his parents could agree on didn't happen that often at his house. So he wasn't taking any chances.

Sam looked up the web site for their rafting company. There he found several terrifying pictures in the former rafters section. Some were even worse than he'd seen on TV. *These people look like they're fighting for their lives*, he thought. In one picture, the rocks looked ten times bigger than the helpless looking rubber raft trying to make it in between. And the smiles on the faces of the people he saw looked more like they were gritting their teeth, not having fun. He even thought the expressions were frozen on their faces from total terror.

Sam decided to call Tyler.

"Hey."

"Hi," Sam said. "You got a minute?"

"I got tons of 'em."

"Whadaya think of this trip?"

"Looks like a suicide mission to me," Tyler said.

"No kidding. All of a sudden I'm starting to see some terrible things on TV and the computer about rafting."

"Like what?"

"Like people who're about to die, that's what."

Tyler sat silent for a few moments. Then he said, in a softer voice than usual, "If you wanna know the truth, I'm scared to death."

Sam sat up a little straighter and leaned forward. "You are?"

"Sure I am, but I didn't want to look like a sissy to you guys. I figured if *you* thought it looked okay…"

"But you should never do something, especially if it's dangerous, just because of someone else. You gotta decide for yourself."

"I know. I just thought that because there'd be grownups that make these trips all the time, we'd be okay, because what could happen to a couple of kids, right?"

Sam leaned back in his chair again. "Well, I hope so."

"What do you mean by that?"

"I'm not sure."

"Great," Tyler groaned. "Now you tell me."

"What's that supposed to mean?"

"It means that I know Tony a whole lot better than you do. He's done some crazy things, that's all."

Sam let out a deep breath. "All I know is I have a bad feeling something might happen."

Tyler didn't say another word. He didn't have to because right now, Sam's heart had already started pounding at double speed.

CHAPTER 3
PACKING FOR ADVENTURE

The next two days became a blur as Sam worked madly to get everything ready. He tried to put the dangers of a rafting trip out of his mind. Then he couldn't believe that his Sunday school lesson for the week was about Noah and the flood. The thought of all that rain made him shiver. He remembered hearing about a freak rainstorm years ago in the Colorado Rockies that sent water from a small creek rushing out of its banks. In less than an hour it raged as a wall of water through the canyon, killing several hikers and campers.

On the way home from church, his father had the oldies station on the radio and Sam heard a song about troubled waters. And then, after supper, he found his parents in the den where they were watching a movie about some poor farmer battling to save his crops from a rapidly rising river.

"I think somebody's trying to tell me something," he

whispered. *At least there aren't any fish in the river big enough to try to swallow me like Jonah...are there*?

He had a feeling, deep down in his stomach that felt a lot like when he, Tony, and Tyler had gotten caught up in the violent storm that had smashed their catamaran. *What if something like that happened again*, Sam wondered.

He tried everything he could think of to go to sleep that night but all he could see in his mind were rafts full of people falling into an angry river. *They couldn't be that crazy*, he thought. Then he remembered how proud Tony was that he and his uncle had already gone hang gliding. That idea kept him awake until the middle of the night.

The next morning he and his mother hit the shopping trail to pick up more of the things he still needed on his list.

"We'll be done by noon," she told him, as he slammed his door and they began backing out of the driveway.

"Great. Then I can finish packing."

"This is a big trip, probably the biggest you've ever taken."

"I know. I can't believe Tony's uncle is paying for everything."

"Sure is nice of him. And you listen carefully to everything he tells you. It's always a good idea to learn from people who have experience in something you know nothing about."

After a nervous laugh, Sam said, "I plan to."

Their first stop was at the drug store. Sam needed sunscreen, a new toothbrush, a travel-sized tube of toothpaste, and sunglasses. Next they went to the mall to buy socks, shorts, flip-flops, and an adventure hat. Actually, it looked more like a fishing hat, but this one would keep the sun off the back of his neck.

After that, they drove to a sporting goods store because Sam wanted a compass and a waterproof case for his binoculars.

Sam's mother looked up toward the ceiling. "You'd think you boys were going to the Amazon Jungle instead of the Colorado River." Before leaving the sporting goods store, she also bought Sam a new plastic poncho.

"How am I going to carry all this stuff on the river?" he asked.

His mother shook her head. "Glad it's you and not me."

They were back home in time for lunch. Sam made himself a gigantic peanut butter and grape jelly sandwich on two pieces of thick, whole wheat bread.

"I wonder what kind of food you'll have on the river?" his mother said, as she handed him a glass of juice.

Sam held up one hand because he had to chew a little more before he could answer. "I read on the website that they always serve some pretty amazing food, and lots of it."

"Like what?"

He set down his sandwich. "Steaks, fish, pork chops, and the biggest breakfasts you can imagine."

After lunch, Sam went to the computer so he could read a few more details about the trip. As he looked at the different pages, he could hardly believe that in just a couple more days he'd be in a raft on the same river, just like the people in the pictures.

Around one o'clock that afternoon, Tyler came over and

they went to Sam's room.

"I didn't expect to see you again until we leave tomorrow," Sam told him.

"Me either. But I want you to do something."

"Sure. What's up?"

Tyler motioned for them to go over to Sam's computer.

"Now what?"

"Before I came over I did a search. Type in 'river rafting deaths' and see what happens."

Sam did that and up popped several links to sites telling some awful stories about people who had died on trips just like the one they were about to take. "This doesn't prove anything."

Tyler pointed at the screen. "It proves you can die out there."

"Sure, but people make mistakes."

"And who can make mistakes better than a guy who doesn't even know what mistakes to make?"

"That's why we have guides."

Tyler pointed at the screen again. "You think those guys didn't?" He read the first couple of lines from a story where an entire raft of people disappeared on the river. "Look. It says their bodies were never found."

Sam rubbed his forehead. "Well, it also says that the people were drinking. We already know that makes you stupid."

"They couldn't all have been doing that." Tyler pointed to another story. "Look at this one where the two seventy-five-year-old women drowned."

Sam smiled. "Are you comparing us to a couple of seventy-five-year-old women? Come on!"

"I'm just sayin'."

"Maybe they couldn't swim."

"I'm tellin' you, it's gonna be dangerous."

"Sure it is. So we have to be extra careful then, and listen to instructions. I think we'll be safe."

"I hope so, but I'm still worried."

After Tyler left and Sam had a chance to think about what his friend had said, he had to admit that he felt a little wobbly in the knees, too, each time he thought about the dangers. So he tried to stop doing that.

For the second night in a row, after Sam had gone to bed, he didn't get much sleep. He kept tossing in his bed as he survived dream after dream of near-miss collisions between his raft and giant boulders with angry faces on them. As he passed each one, they turned toward him with their loud, evil laughs that echoed through the canyon above the roar of the rapids.

Some of the trees in one of his dreams tried to reach down with their branches and grab him. The dreams were worse than the scariest movie he had ever seen. By morning he was just relieved to see the sun again. *At least I know I'm still alive*, he thought.

When he went to the kitchen for breakfast, his father already had the car loaded with Sam's duffel bag and equipment. They planned to meet at Tony's house. Then they'd cram everything in one car and be on their way.

"This is gonna be the longest trip I've ever taken in a car,"

Tony said. "Usually my dad and I fly, but we can't this time."

"How come?" Tyler asked.

"Because of all this junk we have to take for the river," Sam said.

"I don't even know where we're going," Tyler complained.

"My dad already punched it into his GPS. It takes two days. We even have to drive at night some"

"And I looked at a map," Sam said. "I wrote down the places we'll drive through." He took a card out of his pocket. "Let see, we start in Florida."

"No duh," Tony said.

"Then we go through Georgia, Tennessee, Missouri, Kansas, Colorado, and then finally Utah."

"That many?" Tyler asked. "I've never been out of the state before."

Tony pulled out more papers. "My uncle's been sending me emails about every five minutes. I know there's one with the trip information on it."

"I'm taking you to a place called Moab, Utah," Tony's father told them.

"Moab?" Tyler gasped. "I thought that was a Bible place."

"Same name…different place."

Tyler sighed. "Whew. And I was worried about Yugoslavia."

"Here it is," Tony said. "Southwest of Moab, Utah is one of America's wildest canyons. Located in the remote southeast corner of the state, rafters travel through the Canyonlands National Park."

"Sounds okay so far," Sam said.

"Wait, it gets better."

"What do you mean by better?" Tyler asked in a timid voice.

"The first part of the trip is slow and lazy. We can swim along the way, relax, sleep in the raft. Whatever we want."

"I like the sound of that," Tyler said. "It does seem better."

"That's not the *better* part."

Tyler stiffened up. "Why did I know that?"

"Next you have to get ready for Cataract Canyon."

Tyler looked toward the sky. "And what's that?"

"That's where the Green and Colorado Rivers come together. It's where all the fireworks start."

Tyler looked back at Tony. "Fireworks?"

"Rapids…big ones," Tony said as he held his arms up and down as far apart as he could stretch.

"I read the peak season is May and June," Sam said.

"What does peak mean?" Tyler asked.

"The *most* fireworks."

"Ohhh…I don't feel so good," Tyler complained. Then he snapped his fingers. "Wait a minute. This is July. Isn't that supposed to be safer than May and June?"

"This is the time of year when you should usually see what they call class four and five rapids. But I read about the weather they've been having in Utah this summer."

"And?" Tyler asked.

"There've been a lot of heavy rains up river. I emailed my uncle about it, and he said the river might be even more angry than usual."

Tyler's voice quivered. "A river can get angry?"

"Well, the ocean sure did when we went diving," Tony reminded them.

Sam smiled. "I think we're in for a pretty wild ride, and I… can't…wait!"

"Did we have to come now?" Tyler groaned.

"We do if you want the greatest adventure," Tony said, with one of his scariest voices.

"Oh, right," Tyler said.

"Anyway, the worst, I mean the greatest rapids are supposed to be on the Colorado right after the two rivers meet. It should really be something!" Tony said.

"Then what?" Tyler asked.

"Well, if we survive all the rocks and stuff, then we travel on till we get to a place called Lake Powell."

"And that's where I'll be waiting to pick you boys up," Tony's father said, as he walked up to the car.

"Am I ever gonna be glad to see you again," Tyler said. "In fact, I think I'll be glad to see anybody by then."

"We're riding in the big rafts with oars," Tony said.

Tyler gulped. "Do we hafta know how to use them?"

"Not really. My uncle said our raft would be at the end of the line. He's gonna tie a rope from ours to the raft in front of us. That way, the more experienced rafters and guides will just pull us through the rapids safely."

"Sort of like at a theme park ride," Sam said.

Tony nodded with an evil grin. "All we gotta do is hang on

for dear life."

Tyler sighed. "I don't think I've had this much fun since I broke my leg two years ago."

CHAPTER 4
TO THE RIVER

Since Sam had already lived in so many different places, because his father's work caused the family to move around a lot, he didn't pay too much attention to the states they blasted through. And anyone who has traveled long distances on the Interstate knows you don't get to see much unless you pull off and drive into a town or tourist area. But there was no time for that on this trip. They had an appointment to meet up with the rafting expedition for orientation and instructions, or they'd be left behind.

Sam couldn't keep from thinking about the river adventure ahead, but Tyler was a different story. Often he'd point to something and say, "Look at that!"

Once when he did it, Tony asked, "Why do you keep doing that?"

Tyler slumped back in his seat. "Just because you guys have

traveled all over, doesn't mean I have. I've never even been out of Florida."

"Ever flown on a plane?" Sam asked.

Tyler shook his head and looked down.

Tony glanced up to where his father sat behind the wheel. "Think we'll fly someplace again on one of your trips, Dad?"

His father turned half way back, "It's possible."

Tyler's mood brightened. "You mean it?"

"Why not?"

"And I'd get to fly on a real plane with you and everything?"

"We'll see," Tony's father said.

Tyler whistled. "That'd really be something."

Tony's father had wanted to drive straight through, but for safety, he planned one motel stop into the schedule. Other than that, they continued pounding down the highway. After what seemed like a week, Tony's father finally called out, "Moab, fifty miles."

Sam's heart pumped a little faster when he heard that. He was excited about the trip, but he was more than a little worried, too. After all, this was the first time he'd gone on a big trip without at least one of his parents along. His father took him to a convention once where he got to see all the new toys before they could be found in stores. He had to wear a special badge and everything. But this trip was different. Not even Tony's father would be with them.

"Do we go right out on the water?" Tyler asked.

Tony answered, "We spend the first night on the river."

"We do? Honest?" Tyler gasped.

"Bank, the river...*bank.*"

"Whew," Tyler sighed.

"It's a big campout where we meet all the people who'll be going with us. They also tell us about the rules and go over safety. Besides, you don't want to be out on a river like this in the dark."

"Not so sure I want to be out there in the daylight either," Tyler said. "At least in the night, it'd be too dark to see what was about to kill your bones."

"Then, after breakfast the next day, we head out. We use their tents and a lot of stuff that most other people have to rent. But because my uncle is taking us, it's all free."

"Even the food?" Sam asked.

Tony grinned. "Especially the food."

Tyler whistled. "This must cost some people a fortune."

"See why hanging around with a guy like me can be worth it?" Tony said, with a proud smile. "How much farther, Dad?"

"About ten minutes."

Sam started to feel the same way he'd always felt just before a big test at school. He became real quiet. His stomach fluttered, his hands turned cold, and he felt nervous all over. *Still, this should be fun*, he thought. *Right?* He forced down a hard swallow.

They pulled into an area where other cars were already parked. Sam saw the river not far beyond them as he climbed out. He noticed huge, black rubber boats lined up along the bank. In the parking lot, people were busy unloading their things.

Then they heard a loud yell. "Tony, you crazy kid! Get over here and give your Uncle Harlan a big…slap on the hand."

Tony ran to him and hugged his uncle anyway. Then they walked back to meet the others. Sam stood back a half step as he looked at this giant of a man. His skin was as dark as a pair of brown shoes. His face and hands looked rough, like a scuffed-up football that had been left outside too long. There were tattoos on his arms. Sam didn't like those one bit, but he couldn't help looking at them.

Tony's uncle had wild, bushy hair and a scruffy beard. "This must be Tyler and Sam," his voice thundered.

Sam put out his hand. "Glad to meet you." Tony's uncle grabbed his hand so hard he thought it might break right off. The big man's hand felt rough and strong. Tyler was next and when they shook hands, it looked to Sam like his friend might pass out on the spot. Their gear was quickly unloaded, Tony's father said good-bye, and then he drove away.

After Tony's father had left, his uncle told them to bring their things over to the registration tables so they could sign in. They had brought all their insurance and medical information, just as the instructions said. Those forms had been faxed to Tony's house earlier.

"What did your uncle used to do before this?" Tyler asked.

"A lot of things. First, he was a Marine. Then he worked on a ship that went all over the world. He's raced motorcycles, worked on a cattle ranch…you know, normal stuff like that."

"Normal?"

Tony looked at him. "Well, not everybody lives in a small town like we do. There's a whole world out there, ya know?"

"I guess so."

"Hey," Sam said. "When do we eat? I'm starving."

As soon as he'd said that, someone blew a loud whistle. They walked with the other people to find out what was happening.

Tyler's voice went up a little higher. "Think somebody fell in?"

Tony motioned to his friends. "Come on. Let's go see." The shrill sound of a whistle split the air again, and they ran toward it.

As soon as the rafting group stood in front of Tony's uncle, he said in his loud voice, "My name is Harlan, but most people call me Sarge. Long as you follow the rules we should get along fine. If you don't, I might just drop you off on a river bank for the wild animals to eat."

Tyler gulped, but Tony puffed up with pride.

"Seriously, the river can be a beautiful and a dangerous place, all at the same time. Each raft will have an experienced guide who knows where the danger spots are. Since you don't know those places…listen to your guide. He'll keep you safe. Next, I want you to meet my nephew, Tony. Tony and his two friends Sam and Tyler will be going with us this trip."

They looked around, waved, and smiled nervously.

"We're going to tie their smaller raft to one of the bigger ones at the end of the line. They'll also be carrying some of our supplies, so we don't want *their* raft to get lost."

Several of the people laughed.

"So, tonight let's eat up, and get a good night's rest. The fun begins in the morning."

Tyler looked up at the sky and groaned. "I can hardly wait,"

After a great dinner, Sam and his friends hurried back to get their campsite ready. Even though there had been heavy rains a couple of days earlier, the weather forecast now called for cool nights and warm days. Once their sleeping bags were ready they walked over to the edge of the river. Sam leaned down and put his hand into the water. "Brrr. You wouldn't wanna go swimming for long in that water."

Tyler dipped his hand in. "Yikes! This feels like it came straight from snow up in the mountains."

"I thought the information said we could go swimming," Sam said.

"Who's stopping you?" Tony asked. "Nobody said it had to be warm."

Tyler laughed. "Yeah, like those crazy polar bear people who break through the ice and go swimming up north."

The sun seemed to sink quickly, changing the warm colors into a cool blue. If it hadn't been for a huge campfire, the people would have looked like black cutouts. Along with Tony and Tyler, Sam moved toward the warmth of that fire.

"Joke time!" someone suggested a few minutes later.

"I got one about a river," another man called out.

"Go for it."

"Two mountain men had been fishing all day on opposite sides of a river. It was nearly dark and the first man kept pulling fish out as fast as he could get his line back into the water. The second guy wasn't catching anything so he yelled across, 'Hey! I'd sure like to fish on your side of the river.' The first guy called back, 'Tell you what. I'll shine my flashlight across and you can walk on the little beam of light till you get here.' The second guy shook his head and said, 'You must think I'm pretty stupid. I'd get about half way across and you'll turn your light off.'"

Most of the people groaned or hissed, and not too many laughed.

"Wait," he said. "I got a better one."

"It'd have to be," a voice moaned.

"There was this prospector working his claim on one side of the river. He'd struck gold while a claim jumper watched from the other side. 'Hey you over there,' the second man said. 'How can I get to the other side of this river?' The prospector stopped what he was doing, took off his hat, and scratched his head. Then he looked the claim jumper in the eye and said, 'You're already *on* the other side.'"

Sam laughed when he heard that. *Wonder if there're still any prospectors around here*, he thought.

While Sarge gave out a few final instructions, Sam also noticed that Tony's uncle might have looked a little rough, but he seemed gentle and nice on the inside. Especially the way he made sure everyone would be safe on the river. Then he noticed a frightened look on Tyler's face. "What's the matter with you?" Sam whispered.

His friend looked around and whispered back, "Do you think

there are any of those where we're going?"

"Any what?"

"Prospectors and gold mines."

"I was thinking the same thing, but I don't know. Why?"

"I'd be scared of claim jumpers." His eyes started blinking.

Tony tapped him on the shoulder and that made him jump. "You worry too much."

One of the guides stepped toward the center of the ring of people gathered 'round the fire. "This area was one of the last parts of the United States to be settled by people moving west. Outlaws, like Butch Cassidy and the Sundance Kid, and the Hole in the Wall Gang, used to ride to their hideouts around here after robbing the Colorado mining towns."

Tyler looked to his friends. "Now I *am* scared. And don't you try to talk me out of it this time."

CHAPTER 5

FIRST NIGHT

Except for Lost Island, Sam, Tony, and Tyler had never slept out on the ground like this before. All of the tents and other equipment were already loaded on the rafts so the rafters could leave when the sun came up in the morning.

"I sure hope it doesn't rain while we're asleep," Tyler said.

"There you go, worrying again," Tony said.

Every noise they heard out in the bushes made all three of them sit up and look around. The scariest sound came from a big owl hooting away somewhere in the distance.

After nearly an hour of this, Tony's uncle came by to check on them. He sat down on a tree stump next to their sleeping bags. "How's everybody doing?" he asked.

"Fine if you want to stay awake all night," Tyler said.

"You'll get used to it."

"I keep thinking some wild animal's gonna sneak up and bite

my nose off."

Tony's uncle laughed. "Don't think I've lost any noses out here yet."

"Uncle Harlan, has anybody drowned on one of your raft trips?"

He shook his head. "*I've* never had any. Now that's not to say it doesn't happen, because it does."

"I read about some of those online," Sam told him.

"But we take all the precautions. You'll be wearing life jackets, helmets, and goggles."

"Helmets?" Tyler asked.

"Sure. Those are some pretty hard rocks out there. And with your raft tied to the one in front of you, it should be a lot safer."

"Should be?" Tyler asked.

Tony's uncle nodded.

"What are the rapids like?" Sam asked.

"The river starts out smooth and slow, like you see it now. Gives you a chance to get the feel of your boat and everything. A little farther down the river, we'll hit some smaller patches of rapids. They can be pretty scary for first-timers like yourselves. But those only help you get ready for the big show."

Tyler cleared his throat, but his voice still quivered. "Big show?"

"Once the two rivers come together, that's when the fireworks start."

"That's what I told them," Tony said.

Tyler gulped. "Fireworks?"

"Have you boys ever watched cowboys riding bulls or bucking broncos in a rodeo?"

"Sure. Lots of times," Tony said.

"This is a hundred times worse, only you'll be riding on water. And in a rodeo, the rider just has to stay on for a few seconds before the buzzer." He pointed out toward the dark river. "Out there…there's no buzzer. You have to stay on until the rapids stop."

"Is it really that bad?" Sam asked.

"Depends on how much rain we've had. Up until a couple days ago, it hasn't been too rough this season. But it'll still be wild out there because of the recent storms. That's why I didn't want you to have to worry about helping to steer one of the large rafts. We need bigger people with a lot of experience on the river to do that. Like I said, your raft will be tied right behind one of those guides. All you have to do is hang on. It should be a fun ride for you because you don't have to do anything."

"Yeah, except try not to fall out," Tyler said.

"Your raft has plenty of places to hold on. The three of you will have the best ride because you get to watch what's going on the whole time."

"I'm gonna have my eyes shut tight," Tyler said as he closed them.

"It'll be fun," Tony said. "You guys should've been hang gliding with us. Now *that* was scary."

Tyler shuddered. "No thanks. This'll be scary enough for now."

Tony's uncle stood to leave. "You boys try to get some sleep. We have a long day tomorrow."

After he left, Sam said, "I like your uncle. Does he have any kids?"

"My Mom told me he never got married. That's how come he can go around doing all the crazy stuff he's done."

"I guess that'd be fun for a while, but I think I'd like things a little more safe."

"Maybe so," Tony said, "but I'm pretty sure we left safe back home."

After the long drive no one could stay awake any longer. Uncle Harlan had to wake them up the next morning. "Didn't you hear the whistle?"

Sam rubbed his eyes and sat up. "Wha…what whistle?" he mumbled.

"I blew it three times." Then he lifted it and blew it as hard as he could. He laughed and said, "Sun'll be up soon."

Tyler groaned. "Five more minutes?"

"It's up to you, but I know three boys who are about to miss breakfast if they don't hurry."

That's all they needed to hear. They got ready so fast, Tyler took off running without his shoes. Each of them filled a large, plastic tray with eggs, sausage, toast, and pancakes. Sam and his friends had to eat quickly since they were the last to be served. Soon after breakfast they hurried back to roll up their sleeping bags and load their things onto the smaller raft that would be their new home on this trip.

Sam looked over to see some of the adults easing the larger rafts into the water. “This should really be fun, Tony. Thanks for inviting us.”

“I know, and we get the best seats on the river.”

“The best seat would be along the river...*bank* someplace,” Tyler told them, “watching the rest of these crazy people shooting by.”

They picked up the last of their things and headed for the rafts. Tony’s uncle showed them how to tie everything down so when they did hit rough water, nothing would be lost.

“I saw another group of rafts my first time out here and it was the funniest thing.”

“Why? What happened?” Sam asked.

“Well, they didn’t tie anything down. When they went through the rapids, their stuff started flying out. Then when they tried to grab for it, they stopped holding onto their rafts.”

“Then what?” Tyler asked.

“Then they flew out too. I think it was a pretty short trip for that bunch. All you could see were duffel bags and bobbing heads floating down the river. It really isn’t funny either, because the river can be dangerous.”

“Oh, man.” Tyler sighed.

“You boys lined all your bags with plastic like I wrote you?”

“Yes,” they said, together.

“Good. And make sure to put your sleeping bags and the rest of your things in plastic bags. There’s nothing worse after a long day on the river than trying to climb into a cold, wet, soggy, sleeping bag."

Sam made sure to tie the top of his trash bags extra tight.

"Okay, people. Time to move out."

The rafters followed Sarge's orders. They placed the last of their things into the rafts, climbed in, and pushed away from the bank.

"Good bye, world," Tyler cried as their raft moved away from dry land. The larger raft they'd been tied to pulled them forward.

The first part of the trip was exactly as they expected. The rafts hardly seemed to be moving in the slow, calm waters. People laughed, sang songs, and told stories. Their voices bounced off the water, making lots of funny sounds. Later in the morning, some of the people fell asleep while others decided to take a dip in the cold water. They didn't stay in very long.

The guides had said there would be a few rapids later on but that those would be practice runs for when the Colorado and Green rivers met. One of the guides, Cal, had been on every run Uncle Harlan made on the river since he started taking people through the rapids. He liked to wear a big hat with a feather sticking up on one side. Cal almost always had a toothpick in his mouth. "Keep an eye out for mule deer, egrets, blue heron, and desert big horn sheep," Cal said.

"And hawks," another added.

For several miles outside of Moab, the rafters drifted along while other people slipped through the water in their kayaks. Still others created their own fury in the calm waters with jet skis. But before the day was over, the rafters got their first taste of rapids, even though these were only rated as a low class two. The really big stuff would be twice that high, they had been warned.

The group stopped along the river for lunch. Then, near the end of the day, the rafts were beached again so the rafters could set up camp for the night.

"Our forecast is for possible showers tonight so we'll put up all the tents," Tony's uncle announced. "After that you can get in line for dinner."

Sam and his friends didn't know much about putting up a tent so they helped the other, more experienced campers to do that. As the sun began to set they heard the mournful sounds of coyotes calling in the distance. That made Sam shiver slightly.

"What about rattlesnakes around here?" Tyler asked.

"You don't bother them and they won't bother you," Cal said.

"Does that mean they're around here?"

"Yes, they are."

Tyler jumped right up into Tony's arms. "Really?" he asked as his eyes blinked again and his head jerked twice.

Immediately every stick and shadow on the ground started looking like snakes to Sam. He began watching each step he took.

"Now, tomorrow," Uncle Harlan said, "you can expect to see your first class three rapids. Those will be rough enough to shake up your breakfast so be on your guard. The moment you lose your fear and respect for this river is the time when the river will make you pay."

The coyotes continued their yapping far into the night. Sam scrunched down a little deeper into his sleeping bag, happy that he and his friends weren't lost someplace along the river all alone tonight.

That'd be the worst, he thought.

CHAPTER 6

SEPARATED FROM THE OTHERS

The rapids from the first day had thrown everyone around a bit, but those were nothing compared to what they saw the next day. These class three rapids made their own sound in the distance. The roar could be heard bouncing off the rocks and canyon walls on both sides of the river.

Tyler's head popped up a little higher, his eyes got bigger, and he strained to look ahead of their raft. "What's that sound?"

Sam's heart started beating faster. He remembered what it had felt like, the first time he waited in line for a new super roller coaster at a theme park in one of the cities where he used to live; the kind where his feet dangled helplessly in thin air. The ride he was thinking of flew him upside down at least six times before the terror was over. His thoughts went back to the screams he'd heard from people already flying through the air. But it was the roar of the coaster he remembered most, and he couldn't forget the feeling in his stomach as the ride stopped right in front of him. There was the brief hiss when all the doors opened. When he'd sat down, an operator came by, shut the door to his car, checked his shoulder belts, and then signaled to the man at the controls. A red button was pushed, and by that time it was too late to turn back.

Now he heard the same kind of roar he'd heard back then, people screamed in the rafts up ahead, and Sam knew for sure, it was too late again.

"Hang on," Cal said from the raft directly in front of them.

Sam reached up to make sure the rope was tight. He looked back and noticed that even though Tony would never admit it,

from the look on his face, he was terrified. His hands couldn't have held any tighter to the safety ropes, because all of his knuckles were white and sticking out, and the color had gone out of his face. Sam also knew that Tyler was probably already having a near-death experience, watching his young life pass before his eyes, which were blinking again.

"If we ever got loose from that raft in front of us, we'd be in real trouble," Sam shouted to his friends. With a shaking hand he re-checked the strap on his helmet while hanging onto the raft with the other. "You guys hold on tight," he warned.

Tyler's trembling voice called back, "Don't worry, it'd take a doctor to cut *me* loose."

They entered the next rapids at a speed that felt more like a powerful motor was pushing them, not simply a moving river. The beginning of the ride reminded Sam of the roller coaster he'd thought about when he first heard the sound, but the difference was that the raft he was sitting in had no wheels or track. It could go wherever it wanted to…and it did.

As they rolled around a sharp turn and the raft in front of them, the very one they were connected to, moved into position to shoot through the narrow passage, the last raft, containing Sam, Tony, and Tyler, became caught up on a small log wedged into the rocks. For an instant they stopped still. Then the worst thing happened. They all heard a loud snap like someone cracking a whip. After that their raft began moving again. That's when Sam reached out and pulled on the rope. Its other end quickly came to the surface.

Sam gulped. "Hey, guys. We aren't hooked to that raft anymore."

"Are you sure?" Tony gasped.

Sam held up the broken rope. "Look."

"Oh, no. Now what?" Tyler cried out.

"Now we hang on," Tony yelled.

Already the other rafts had raced out of sight at high speed. Sam figured that with the roar of the water, no one even knew what had happened yet, or that they were already this far behind. "Grab an oar," he ordered.

His friends quickly found one. "Now what?" Tyler screamed.

"I saw it on TV before we left home. We can use them to keep us off the rocks."

Sam was sure there were still several large rapids ahead. With the rumble from the water, it was almost impossible to hear anything else. They made it through the first narrow spot, but then turned all the way around as their helpless raft approached the next one. That's when the side of their raft hit a sharp stick and Sam heard a blast of air escape from the chamber on the same side. It reminded him of that roller coaster door opening. Immediately the raft began taking on water. It spun around again in the raging waters, only to rip a giant hole in the back air chamber.

"We gotta get this thing to shore," Tony shouted.

"I know," Sam answered as he battled the foaming water. "I'm trying."

By now they were sitting in water up to their stomachs, and

it was as cold as a glass of ice water. Sam knew that if they didn't get off that river, they could smash into the rocks with nothing left of the raft to protect them. "I see a place to the right. Use your oars to steer us that way."

Just then Tyler's oar wedged in between two sharp rocks. He tried to hold onto it, but the oar snapped in two, leaving a useless short piece of wood in his hands. Sam and Tony continued their struggle against the powerful force of the river until what was left of their raft finally moved out of the main current and into calmer waters.

"I think we can make it to that place over there." Sam pointed to an area where the rocks opened up into a small lake. They paddled as fast as they could toward that opening. The water became almost completely quiet after they passed through the narrow opening.

Tyler held his head in his hands. "Nobody's ever gonna find us out here."

"I'll bet they're looking for us already," Tony said.

"Sure," Sam added. "Most likely they saw us break loose right away, and beached their rafts." He looked around the banks of the river. "Probably heading this way on land right now."

"I hope you're right," Tyler said, without looking up.

Sam looked around on both sides of this smaller part of the river. "Let's get over to that sandy beach before this whole thing sinks."

They paddled to the place where he had pointed, jumped out of their damaged rubber raft, and pulled it up on shore.

"First we gotta see what we have left," Sam said.

"I was in the back," Tyler said, "and I didn't see anything fall out."

"Yeah," Tony said. "That's because your eyes were shut the whole time."

After going through everything, Sam found that they still had a tent, all their bags of clothes, and several cases of food, shovels, and a few things that belonged to the other rafters.

"At least we've got food," Sam said. "Our raft was even carrying extra food for some of the other people."

"And we've got a place to sleep," Tony said as he held up their tent. "It could be worse."

"Not much," Tyler whimpered.

"We'd better set up a camp before it gets dark," Sam told them. "And let's hang up the wet stuff while we've still got the sun."

"Do you think your uncle will turn around and come back looking for us?" Tyler asked.

Tony threw back his head and laughed. "You don't turn around on a river like this and go back up. You go where the river takes you."

"Oh, right."

"They'll have to send someone down again or look for us from the air," Tony said.

Tyler started scanning the clouds and blue sky.

"But they don't even know where they lost us," Sam said.

Tony looked high up to the rocks on both sides. "I know."

After checking to make sure the inside of his duffel bag had stayed dry with the plastic bag lining, Sam began opening the heavy cases from their raft.

"What are you looking for?" Tyler asked.

"Matches. You guys start picking up dry wood. We need a fire tonight. After I find the matches, I'll help you."

"What about snakes?" Tyler asked.

"Don't pick those up," Tony joked.

"Just be careful. If you see a stick, make sure it really is a stick before you grab it," Sam said.

Tyler stepped into the flat raft. "How 'bout I look for the matches."

"Get going, Tyler. We have a lot to do." While the others searched for firewood, Sam found cans of soup, ravioli, peaches, peas, stew, corn, potatoes, and meats. *Everything we need*, he thought. Their raft also had cooking pots and pans, plates, cups, forks, spoons, and soap for washing dishes.

A few minutes later, his friends returned with the first load of wood. "We found a dead tree back there with all the wood we need," Tony told him. "Come on." They hurried to bring back as much firewood as they could carry or drag.

Sam rubbed his hands together to get rid of the sand and tree bark on them. Then he wiped them on his pants. "Next we have to try to set up our tent."

"I watched them do that last night," Tony said. "I think we can figure it out." But putting up that tent made them feel more like clowns in the circus as they fell all over each other, got tangled in the ropes, and watched the tent fall down three times before they finally got it right.

"That looks pretty good," Tyler said, with a little less worry. "What's next?"

"I think we should take a look around this place and see if there's any way we can get out of here."

"Well our raft's dead. We won't be getting out that way," Tony said, as he pointed toward the river.

"I was thinking of trying to hike out," Sam said.

"But we could be a zillion miles from anywhere," Tyler said.

"It doesn't mean we shouldn't try."

Tyler sat down on a large boulder. "I think we should stay right here till help comes."

"And after all our food runs out?" Sam said.

"Are you tryin' to cheer me up?" Tyler complained.

"I only want to do what's best. We have no radio. Nobody knows where we are…"

Tyler interrupted. "*We* don't even know where we are."

The sun was beginning to slip away. Soon it would be completely down, plunging the area into darkness. Sam did his best to sound confident. "I don't think we're in any serious danger," Just then a coyote began howling in the distance, joined by a second and then a third.

Tyler shuddered. "Wish I knew if *they* knew that."

CHAPTER 7
CLANK IN THE DARK

After the tent was up and their things were stored inside, Sam built a fire. He'd found matches packed in one of the food containers. He got a blaze going just before dark.

"How many matches do we have?" Tyler asked.

Sam put them in his jacket pocket. "Plenty. But we'd better drag the raft over here and cover our firewood."

"What for?"

"It feels like rain."

"It's kinda creepy out here," Tyler said. "No streetlights, or cars, no houses, and no people either…at least I hope there aren't any."

Tony walked over and tossed more wood on the fire. "I like you guys okay. I mean, we're best friends and everything, but right now I wouldn't mind seeing a few more people around besides just us."

"So would I," Sam said.

"You'd think there'd be more rafters on the river. How come none of them camped in here for the night?" Tony asked.

"Remember how we got in here?" Sam said.

"Well, we did have to row pretty hard," Tony said, "but I thought that's only because our raft was going flat."

Sam looked out at the river. "I just don't think all those rafts could have made it in here, at least not past the rocks we came through."

"Look around you," Tyler said. "There's nothing here. And it was too early in the day to stop."

"He's right," Tony said. "It's a long trip. Rafters have to stay on schedule."

"Does your uncle carry a radio?" Sam asked.

"I think so, but like Tyler said, probably no one knows when they lost us or where we are." He looked out toward the water. "It's a long river."

Sam pulled out a cooking pan. "Who's hungry?"

Tyler put his hand up to his stomach. "I'm starving."

"Me, too," Tony said.

They opened two cans of beef stew and a box of biscuits that were already made. Sam grabbed paper plates out of one case, and plastic forks from another. He had placed rocks in the fire and now he set a pan on top of those. In a third case he also found juice boxes, bottled water, and cookies.

"This looks like a great dinner," Tony said, rubbing his hands together.

Sam and his friends ate like three pigs, including a few grunts. They wiped food from their faces, and smeared that on their clothes. In no time, they'd eaten all the stew, biscuits, and cookies.

Tyler stretched, patted his stomach, and asked, "How do we clean up?"

Sam looked back toward the river. "The dishwasher is right over there. And we can burn the paper junk."

"I think I could live out here," Tyler said with a smile. "No dishes to wash."

Sam held up the pot. "Except for this." Then Sam looked into the flames from their campfire. "I don't know," he said. "I just feel safer by a fire."

"Me, too," Tyler said as he moved a little closer to the heat.

"What's the plan?" Tony asked as he tossed another stick into the fire. Sparks flew up and were carried even higher, like hundreds of glowing fireflies, into the air.

Sam looked at him. "After we've eaten, the best thing for us to do is get some sleep. Then first thing in the morning, we have to find a way out of this place."

"But where do we go?" Tyler asked, as his eyes darted all around.

"That's right," Tony said. "I looked at a bunch of maps before we left home. There isn't anything for miles in any direction except wilderness. That's one of the reasons they have guides."

"So whadda we do, Sam?" Tyler asked.

Sam warmed his hands near the dancing flames. "This fire is

a good start. If anyone *is* looking for us, they might spot it from the sky."

"Except we're in this little bitty spot," Tyler said. "Who's gonna look down and say, 'Hey, that must be them down there by that wimpy little fire?'"

"Got any better ideas?"

"I do," Tyler said, "but it's too late for that now."

"For what?" Tony asked.

"I think it'd been a better idea if I'd gone to Yugoslavia."

Sam let out a deep breath. "Well, we're here now. We have to make the best of it. Let's keep the fire going bright till we go to sleep. In the morning we'll have to hike around and try to find our way out."

Just then, something ran behind them in the dark. Its feet made a galloping sound. All three boys dove into the tent, then spun around to see what they'd heard. They poked their heads out of the tent flap…nothing more.

"What was that?" Tyler asked in a whisper.

"Probably a coyote," Tony said.

"More like a wolf," Tyler said.

Sam slipped back into the tent and started opening a couple of the cases again.

"What are you looking for?" Tony asked.

"A flashlight. I saw one when I was getting the food out." He felt around in the dark until his hand hit something. "Here it is." When he turned it on, the whole tent lit up.

"Much better," Tyler sighed. "Shine it outside and see what

that thing was."

Sam moved back up to the flaps, opened one, and began searching around their campsite with the bright beam from his flashlight. Suddenly the light stopped moving. "There's your wolf."

"Where?" Tyler screamed as he dove under his sleeping bag. When the others started laughing he slowly crawled back out. "What's so funny?"

Tony laughed. "Take a look."

When he did, Tyler saw the jackrabbit his friends were watching. "Well, it could have been a wolf."

Tony caught his breath. "Sure it could, Tyler." Then he fell on his back, rolled around, and laughed harder.

"He probably smelled our stew," Tyler said. That made Tony laugh even more.

After a few minutes, they crawled back out of the tent and finished eating a few more cookies. Then Tyler asked, "How we gonna get that pan clean?"

"We?" Sam asked. He picked it up and headed toward the river. "I'll soak it in water overnight. Then it'll be easy in the morning." When he found the matches earlier, he also pulled out a bag with cleaning materials. He'd set aside a sponge and some dish soap for when he went to the river to wash the pot in the morning. Since the stew juice was still fresh, he was pretty sure it would be easy to clean.

"Let's keep the cans in a trash bag, too." Sam said. "We don't want to mess this place up." When he came back from the river, he put more wood on the fire. The flames flared up again, their light flickering on the rocks and bushes all around the campsite. "Might as well get to bed," he said.

"Yeah," Tyler complained. "It's not like we could watch TV or anything."

"Is it just me?" Tony asked, "or do the coyotes sound louder to you now?"

They listened a little longer. Then Tyler said, "Louder, definitely louder."

"We should be safe in the tent," Sam said.

"Should be?" Tyler asked. "How 'bout *will* be?"

Once the fire was going full blast, Sam and his friends crawled into their tent, tied the flaps closed, zipped up the screen, and slid into the sleeping bags.

"How many batteries do we have?" Tyler asked.

"A few. Why?" Sam asked.

"Does Tyler need a night light?" Tony teased.

"Just go to sleep, you guys." As Sam lay flat on his back, he couldn't see anything except for the glow from their fire. It made him feel safe for the first few minutes, until something terrible happened. At first, they only heard it in the distance.

"What's that?" Tyler asked. "And don't tell me it's a rabbit because I hear a bell…definitely a bell."

In a spooky voice Tony said, "I hear it, too."

"Stay still and be quiet," Sam told them in a whisper. No sooner had he said that than they heard the sound of heavy breathing, and it was coming closer and closer to their tent.

"I don't like this," Tyler whispered.

"Shhh."

Something moved in between the tent and the orange flames flickering from the campfire.

Their eyes widened as a giant shadow moved across the front of their tent. Sam even thought his heart stopped beating for just an instant.

"The thing must be ten feet tall," Tony said.

Tyler's high-pitched voice cracked. "Think it might be Big Foot?"

"And what's with the bell?" Sam whispered.

All three boys trembled, and their teeth chattered as the shadow slowly glided over their tent. Then the bell faded into the distance.

"Go see what it is," Tyler said.

"You go," Tony told him.

"I'm not going out there."

"Well I'm not either."

They stayed in their sleeping bags and continued shaking, as if they'd seen a ghost. No one wanted to fall asleep, but in time, they all did.

Later that night, Sam was awakened by another strange sound. At first he wasn't sure what it was. Then he whispered, "Rain?" He slipped out of his bed and pushed the flap open just a crack. The fire was nearly out. He pushed his hand out into the darkness, and felt raindrops. *Glad we covered the wood*, he thought.

By morning the rain had stopped, but the sand was still wet. Sam hurried out into the cold to get a warm fire going again. Then he began looking for something he could make for breakfast. From one of the cases, he pulled out cartons with pancake mix ready to cook. He found a frying pan and set it on the rocks in his fire.

His friends didn't come out of the tent until they smelled food. "What's for breakfast, Mom?" Tyler asked.

"Pancakes…I think."

"Great," Tony said. "How'd you keep such a good fire going all night?"

"I didn't. The rain put it out."

"It rained?" Tyler asked. He shook his head. "Never heard a

thing."

"I did," Tony said. "You snore."

Sam started flipping the pancakes in his hot pan. "Since we covered the wood last night, it's dry now."

Tyler grinned. "Good thing I thought of that."

"After we eat, and clean up, we should take a look around. Then we can come up with a plan."

Again, they would have embarrassed any parent by the way they ate.

With his mouth crammed full of pancakes, Tyler mumbled, "I think food just tastes better outdoors, don't you?"

Sam nodded as he dropped in a package of link sausages. They began sizzling as soon as they hit the hot pan, and the aroma made his mouth water.

"Hey," Tony said. "What are those?" He pointed to the dirt.

Sam looked down. "Tracks from something."

"They look like a small horse," Tyler said.

"Don't forget," Tony said. "There's deer and rams and stuff out here."

Sam scratched his head. "Yeah? Then what about that bell we heard?"

CHAPTER 8
TRACKS IN THE MUD

Sam served more breakfast as they sat on logs.

Tyler lifted one of his pancakes. "Kinda burnt around the edges, aren't they?"

"Better than starving," Tony mumbled through another mouthful.

"After we finish, we can follow those hoof prints and see what made them," Sam said.

"That's the stupidest thing I've ever heard," Tyler said.

"Why?"

"This place is lousy with wild animals. You think we're gonna follow them back to some kind of ranch or something?"

"Hey," Sam said. "I hadn't thought about that."

"We'll probably wander around in circles out here until we drop dead."

"We've still got plenty of food and a river full of water. I don't think we'll die any time soon."

Tyler stomped his foot. "I hate it out here. I wish I'd never come on this dumb trip."

"I'm starting to wish you hadn't either," Tony said.

"Come on," Sam said. "There's no reason to start fighting. We have to pull together if we ever hope to find our way out of this mess."

"Do you think our parents know we're lost yet?" Tyler asked.

"Let's try to think about other things."

"Like what?"

"I think we should follow the tracks until noon. If we don't find anything, we can eat lunch and try again."

Tyler looked to Sam. "And if we do find something?"

"Depends on what it is. For all we know there *could* be a town near here."

Tyler shook his head and looked down. "I'm so sure."

"My uncle said that's one of the dangerous things about the trip."

"What?"

"Getting lost."

Tyler threw his hands up. "Well, what'd I tell you guys?"

"I'm following the tracks. I don't care what the rest of you do," Sam told them. He tossed a few things into the tent, closed the flaps, and began walking.

"Hey," Tyler called out. "Wait for us."

Sam didn't even slow down or turn around. When the others caught up with him, he pointed up ahead. "The tracks look like they go over that ridge."

"Good thing it rained," Tony said.

"Why?" Tyler asked.

"It made the ground soft so the tracks are easier to follow."

They continued walking toward a narrow passageway between jagged rocks. It was a difficult climb, but soon they came to the top.

"Hey, we lost the tracks," Tony said as the ground became hard as rock.

"Just keep walking. We might see them again." On the other side of the ridge Sam pointed. "There they are."

Tyler stopped, ducked down, and grabbed Sam's arm. "There *who* is?"

"Not who."

"What?"

"The tracks."

"Oh."

Sam led the way, following the tracks again until they came to an even steeper path. Tony looked nearly straight up between more rocks. "I don't know if we can make it up there."

"We gotta try," Sam told him.

Like three mountain goats, they picked their way through the dangerous rocks. Just before reaching the top, Sam heard something. "Get down," he said.

"Get down? But we just climbed all the way up here," Tyler said.

"Quiet." After Sam said that, they all heard the same sound.

"It's the bell," Tony whispered.

Slowly they crawled up to the very top of the ridge and peered out from behind a rocky ledge.

"There you are, girl," a scratchy voice said. "I've been looking for you all morning. Where you been?"

Sam's heart pounded. Who could that be? Was he dangerous? Should they sneak back to camp? These and several more questions raced through his head. "You stay here. I'm gonna take a look," he said. He eased onto his feet and slipped between the last rocks at the top of the ridge. Down below, on the other side of that ridge, he saw a short man wearing dirty brown coveralls with holes in the knees and one of the back pockets, a green plaid shirt, dusty boots, and a wide-brimmed, floppy hat. He was petting the nose of a donkey. As he did that, a bell continued ringing.

Sam stood up and cleared his throat as loud as he could. The man spun around and looked back at him with terror in his eyes. His reaction confused Sam. *Why would he be afraid of me?*

"Who are you?" the man demanded as he moved to the other side of his donkey, picked up a rock, and looked back at Sam. "And how did you get in here? Nobody's supposed to be back this far."

Sam blinked and swallowed hard first. "I…"

"They've got me blocked in here. I haven't been able to get out for two weeks."

"Who? Who's got it blocked?"

The man pointed away from the river. "They do." He looked

back to Sam and ducked down a little. “Are you alone?”

“No,” Sam said.

“Tarnation!” the little man said.

“There are two others with me.”

Quickly the man hid behind the donkey’s head. “Well you can’t have it. I won’t let you.”

“Can’t have what?”

“Shhh. They might hear us.”

Sam turned to his friends and whispered. “I think he’s been out in the sun too long. He’s talking crazy talk.”

“Who is he?” Tony asked.

“He seems to own the donkey, I think.”

“What’s he doing out here?” Tyler asked.

“I don’t know, but he looks scared of me.”

Tyler laughed. “You?”

“He hasn’t seen you guys yet. Come on up.”

Tyler and Tony made the final climb to the top of the ridge and stood beside Sam. When they did that, the old man stood up straight, came back around to the front of the donkey, and dropped the rock he’d been holding. “Why… you’re just boys.”

“Yes, sir,” Sam said.

“Well, I thought you were with those other guys. Where’d you little tumbleweeds come from?”

Sam pointed toward the river. “Back there.”

“How’d you do that?”

“We were on a raft trip,” Tony said.

“Where’s the rest of your party?”

Tyler looked at him. "It was no party. We were with a bunch of people going through the rapids and we almost got killed."

"Then what happened to the rest of them?"

"It isn't what happened to *them*," Sam told him. "It's what happened to us. Our raft was tied to the one in front of us, but we came loose when the rope broke."

The dusty man took two steps toward them. "You mean you're out here all alone?"

Sam nodded.

"This is a very dangerous place. Especially since I discovered..." He stopped short and looked all around. "Are you sure there's nobody else with you?"

Sam sighed. "I wish we did have some grownups, but we don't. It's just us."

"Yeah, my uncle takes people down the river. He's gonna be very upset when he finds out we aren't on the other end of that rope."

The little man rubbed his stomach. "Do you have any food?"

"Plenty," Sam told him. "Don't you?"

"I shoot a rabbit now and again, but I haven't had any supplies for over two weeks. That's because they won't let me out so I can get to the store."

"Who won't?" Sam asked.

The man pointed again, only harder with his finger this time. "Them!"

Sam and his friends looked all around, but they didn't see anyone.

"Follow me to my camp. We can talk there."

"You have a campsite out here, too?" Tyler asked.

"Yes, sonny, I do. Me and Lucky."

"Who's Lucky?"

"My donkey here. If it wasn't for old Lucky, I would never have found it."

"We don't believe in luck," Sam said.

"Well, sir, then you ain't met my Lucky. Why, that donkey's been struck by lightning and got right back up…twice. She was bit by a rattler and just kept on walkin' like nothin' happened. And she's the one that sniffed out my gold mine." He quickly covered his mouth before another word could slip out, and looked around again. "Wasn't s'posed to say the 'g' word."

"Your donkey found a gold mine?" Tyler said.

"'Course, she had to step in the hole first. Nearly broke her good leg."

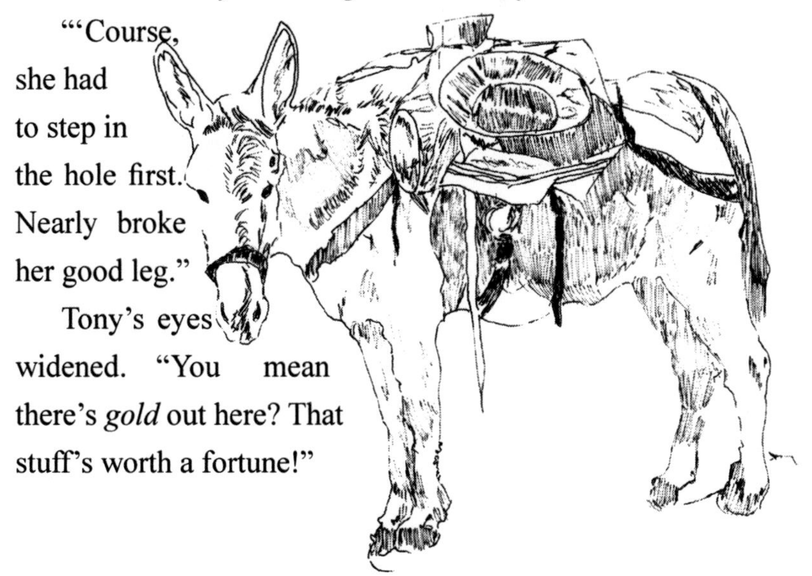

Tony's eyes widened. "You mean there's *gold* out here? That stuff's worth a fortune!"

CHAPTER 9
SCARY BIKER GANG

The old man held a finger up to his lips. "Shhh." Then he looked around to see if anyone had heard when Tony yelled out "gold!"

"Who are you looking for?" Sam asked.

"Let's go to my campsite. We can talk there."

There wasn't much choice but to follow when the old prospector began walking away with his donkey. "What's your names?"

"I'm Sam, this is Tony, and that's Tyler over there." Tyler waved.

"My name's Gus. Mighty pleased to meet you boys."

"Same here, Gus."

"It gets lonesome out here all by myself." When Lucky heard that, she began to cry out as only a donkey can. "Now Lucky, you know what I meant."

They hiked through some tall bushes and came to a place beside a wall of rock. The man had built a small cabin with logs and branches. He'd made the roof out of branches, mud, and rocks. Green plants grew out of several places up there. Gus took them inside, and pointed toward the back of the cabin. "There she is."

Sam and his friends looked into the dark. "There what is?" Tyler asked.

Gus reached up and pulled a rope. When he did, part of his roof opened and the sun lit up the inside of the cabin. That's when they saw a large hole in the ground. "It's right down there," he told them. "I keep the mine hid with this cabin over top of it."

"Pretty smart," Tony said.

"Yes sir. All day long I walk around with Lucky, like I'm looking for gold. Then at night, when nobody can see me, I work the mine while they think I'm asleep."

"When *do* you sleep?" Tyler asked.

"I don't…much."

"Who are you hiding from, and who's 'they'?" Sam asked.

"Claim jumpers."

Tyler looked at Gus. "We've heard about guys like that." One of his eyes started twitching.

"They're nothin' but dirty lowdown rotten rats that wait till an old man like me finds gold. Then they swoop in and try to steal it."

"You mean the gold?" Sam asked.

"No, the mine. If they know there's gold, then all they have to do is take some of it to Moab and say it came from their mine."

"Our raft came from Moab," Tony told him. "How do you get there from here?"

"Well, I used to be able to hike out to the main road. Got an ol' truck hid there under some brush and branches. That's how I got my supplies and other stuff in here."

Tony looked at Gus. "Then why don't we all just hike out there and we're safe?"

Gus took off his floppy hat, shook his head, and rubbed the back of his neck. "Because that's where the claim jumpers are hiding, just waitin' to bushwhack me."

Tyler wrinkled his nose. "Bush what?"

"Listen. I don't mean to scare you boys nor nothin', but folks can get killed out here over the gold. We hafta be real careful."

"What do you want us to do?" Sam asked.

"Just act normal. You can walk around here in the daytime, like I do, and help me in the mine at night. I'll even let you keep what you dig out."

"We get to keep gold!" Tyler shouted.

Gus waved his hands at him. "Shhh. We mustn't let the others know about the gold. Then tomorrow we can try to make it to the truck and get out."

Sam looked around the cabin and then back to Gus. "You said you were out of food."

"Almost."

"Will Lucky go with anybody besides you?"

"If you treat her nice."

"Then I was thinking. Why don't we take her down to the river and bring back some of our food?"

"What have you got?"

Tyler smacked his lips. "Everything."

"Splendid. I don't know when I had my last good meal."

"Will you be all right here by yourself?" Sam asked.

Gus laughed and slapped his leg. "Been all right out here by myself most my life. I 'spect I'll be able to make it till you get back."

Sam pointed toward the road. "Won't they wonder who we are?"

"Never come around until the middle of the afternoon. Probably haven't seen you yet."

"We'd better get going then," Sam said. He took Lucky by

the rope tied around her neck. She turned and walked beside him as if they'd been together for years. "We'll be back as soon as we can."

"I'll be here," Gus said, with a laugh. Then he spit on the ground. "Can't go no place."

Sam and his friends hurried off toward their campsite by the river. It was almost as difficult going down the rocky trail as the climb had been getting up. Lucky acted like she was out for a walk on flat ground. Even though Sam and the others slipped and tripped a few times, she never stumbled.

"What do you guys think of Gus?" Tyler asked.

"I like him," Sam answered.

"Me, too," Tony added.

Sam guided Lucky over a ridge of jagged rocks. "We have to help him get up to Moab."

"How we gonna do that?" Tyler asked.

"Not sure yet. But I'm thinking," Sam said.

Soon they walked into their campsite. Everything looked just as they had left it. With extra ropes they tied two of the food cases on Lucky's back and began their return climb up to Gus' mine.

"I can't believe we know where a real gold mine is," Tyler said. "It gives me goose bumps."

"Gus asked us not to talk about it," Sam said.

"Who's gonna hear us? There's nobody out here but us and Gus."

"It's his mine and he asked us to be quiet."

"Okay…I guess. But I'm still excited."

When they came back to the cabin, Gus was nowhere around. In the distance Sam thought he heard the roar of motorcycles. "Somebody's coming," he shouted.

Tyler started jumping up and down, waved his arms, and yelled "Here. We're over here. Help!"

"Be quiet," Gus scolded.

Tony looked around. "Huh? Where are you?"

"Get in here. Hurry." Nothing but a hand stuck out of the door to a storage shed not far from Gus's cabin. "And bring Lucky in here, too."

They hurried into the shed just before several motorcycles stopped on a hill above Gus' camp. The riders revved them up until the sound became so loud, Sam covered his ears.

"It's like that every day." Gus yelled over the rumble. "They're outlaws. They come around just about this time, sit up on that hill, and watch me. Then at night they go away." A twinkle came to his eyes. "That's when I dig."

"We brought our shovels, too," Sam told him. "But why didn't you try to get away in the morning while they're gone?"

"Because they ain't really *gone*, gone. They hide out there in the rocks and brush like buzzards…just waitin' to swoop in and grab me."

"That's what I'm gonna call them," Tyler said. Then he gritted his teeth. "Nothin' but a bunch of dirty ol' buzzards."

"What do you think we should do, Gus?" Sam asked.

"Work in the mine tonight and dig out as much gold as we

can find. Then in the morning, we'll make a run for it."

Sam shook his head. "I've got a better idea."

The old man scratched his head through thin, white hair. "And what's that?"

"What if we stayed here a few more days?"

"Are you serious?" Tyler whined.

"We can work in your mine, like you said. Only, at night, when two are doing that, the other two can go out and work on a couple of surprises for the biker buzzards."

Gus put his hat back on. "What kind of surprises?"

"A few traps and things to kind of slow them down."

Gus looked to Tony, over to Tyler, and then back to Sam. "What do you mean?"

"Look," Sam told him, "I think it's a good idea to try and get out your way, but you said yourself, those are dangerous people out there."

Gus nodded. "That they are."

"Then I say we need a backup plan."

"Whatcha thinkin' about?"

"We work on the traps the first night. On the second night we start getting our raft ready."

"But the raft's flat and full of holes," Tyler said. "How we gonna pump it up?"

"We're not. I saw some logs near our camp...big ones. We'll use those. And Gus, can we have some of your ropes?"

"All you need."

"Great. We'll tie the logs together and cover them with our

old raft."

"I don't think I like this idea," Tyler said.

"You don't have to like it," Tony said in a huff. "And you can stay here if you wanna."

"I didn't say that."

"Then you'll have to do what I tell you," Sam said.

"But why can't we go out and get Gus' truck?" Tony asked.

"Because. Once they know we have the gold, those guys won't stop until *they* have it, and us. And after what I have planned for them, they're gonna want to get their hands on us real bad!"

Tony shook his head. "You know we still have class four and five rapids ahead if we go that way."

"I know, but it's our only hope to escape." Sam looked back in the direction of the water. "It's the river or nothing."

CHAPTER 10
READY FOR A FIGHT

Later that night, Sam split everyone up into two teams. Gus and Tyler would work the mine while he and Tony planned to go out after dark. Before doing that, Sam heated up more stew.

Gus ate it like he'd never seen stew before. Some of the brown juice ran down into his beard. "Best food I've had in days," he said as he wiped his mouth on the sleeve of his dusty shirt. "Thank you, boys."

"It'll be dark soon. I say we work till midnight," Sam said to Gus. "That way we can still sleep for awhile. Then the three of us will take Lucky and start building our raft."

"Sounds good to me," Gus said. After dark he took Tyler with him into the cabin.

Sam saw a lantern come on once they were safely inside. He whispered to Tony, "Let's go." They took their shovels, along with some of Gus' shorter ropes, and headed toward the one and only narrow pass leading out.

"What are we doing out here?" Tony asked.

"First I wanna dig as many holes as we can in the path. Then we'll cover them with branches."

"What if hikers come along and fall in?"

"Hikers don't come back here. Only Gus and the bad guys."

"So you think they'll fall in the holes."

"If they're dumb enough to chase us, they will. That is, if the tree branches don't knock them off their bikes first."

"Tree branches?"

"That's what the ropes are for."

"Huh?"

"We tie one end of our rope to a branch growing across the path. The other end gets tied to a trip rope a little farther up the path."

"Where'd you learn how to do all this?"

"You don't have the only crazy uncle. I have one in Special Forces. You wouldn't believe some of the things those guys can do."

"Like what?"

"For one, they'd be able to find bugs and junk to eat out here."

Tony shuddered. "Really?"

"If it crawls, they can eat it."

"Yuck."

"And they can dig up roots or find other plants that are safe to eat."

Tony shuddered again. "I like my food to come out of a box, a bag, or a can."

"Anyway, my uncle has taught me all kinds of stuff to do. Come on. We'd better get started."

For the next several hours, they dug deep holes into the path. They had to be careful not to make too much noise with their shovels. And it was hard digging in some spots because of all the rocks. Sam did his best to find softer spots where there was only dirt.

After he and Tony had dug six or seven holes, Sam said, "Why don't you go out and find as much dead brush and sticks as you can."

Tony set his shovel on the ground and looked around the area.

"And remember," Sam told him, "snakes live around here."

"Good thing the moon's so bright," Tony said. He made several trips to gather what he could find. Soon he'd stacked two large piles. Then he helped to dig the last holes.

After all the holes were finished, Sam and Tony covered them with sticks, brush, and dirt. When they'd finished, a person wouldn't know any holes were there at all unless they'd dug them in the first place. At least they looked that way in the moonlight.

Farther up the path, Sam picked out strong tree branches for the next hazard. Tony held each branch back while Sam tied it to the trips he made from fish line. He tied the fish line to the section of rope holding a branch, and then stretched it across the path. He tied a special knot that would let go as soon as any pressure pushed against the line. The thin, clear fish line would be hard to see in the daylight. One time a trip went off accidentally and sent Tony flying backward into the bushes.

"What'd you do that for?" he whispered, as he crawled back up to the path, brushing dirt from his clothes.

"Sorry," Sam said. "It just went off by itself. Guess I didn't tie the knot right. The other thing we need to do is put sharp sticks in the path so if those guys do come this way, we'll be able to flatten the tires on their bikes."

"I never knew you were so smart."

Sam smiled. "Neither did I."

Sam took leftover sticks that Tony had found, and broke them into smaller pieces. With a pocket knife, he cut a sharp point on one end of each stick. Then he buried the sticks into the dirt, with the sharp end sticking up.

"You sure no hikers will get hurt on these things?" Tony asked.

Sam shook his head. "Gus told me that nobody except the bike gang has ever come back here in all the years he searched for his mine. I don't see why people would start walking here now." Then he looked at his watch. "Almost time to go. Hurry."

"How come you never told me you knew how to make stuff like this?" Tony asked.

Sam smiled back at him. "Hey, I just moved here, remember? There's a lot of stuff you don't know about me yet."

In the distance they heard a few coyotes again.

"I really hate the sound of those things at night," Tony

whispered. "They give me the creeps. I don't even like 'em in the daytime."

"They shouldn't bother us," Sam told him.

When they'd finished with the last of the sharp sticks, Tony said, "Boy, I wouldn't want to be the one to come down this trail and not know where all these traps were."

"That's the idea," Sam said with a smile. "Come on. Let's get back to the mine."

The moon still gave off a bright light as they made their way back down the path. Sam glanced up and thought, *Full moon. Wouldn't you know it?*

When they reached the cabin, Sam noticed the light inside had gone out. He tapped Tony on the shoulder and they crouched down. Quiet as two mice, they crept toward the door. Sam reached out, touched the handle, and the door suddenly flew open. "Who's out there?" Gus demanded.

Sam grabbed his chest. "It's just us, Gus. Man, you almost scared me to death."

"Sorry, boys. We couldn't see who it was."

"Wait'll I show you guys what I found," Tyler said. When Gus lit the lantern Tyler held out his hand. "See?"

Sam looked down at something glittering in the dim light. "Is that what I think it is?"

"It's real gold," Tyler whispered. "And I get to keep it."

"How did it go out there?" Gus asked.

"Everything's ready. Tomorrow we'll build the raft."

"Splendid!"

"But I need to tell you one thing. When this is all over, we need to come back with you and undo all the traps."

"Yeah," Tony said. "Some hiker could really get hurt."

Gus shook his head. "I told Sam that nobody's ever come out here before those men."

"We still need to do it," Sam said. "Or you could get hurt, too."

They all slept for the rest of the short night in Gus's cabin until the sun came up again. Sam had become sort of the camp cook. So today he made French toast from slices of bread and an egg mix in a carton. Gus had a great place set up for cooking. He'd put part of an outdoor grill across rocks that he stacked up on both sides. A large fire could be built under it with dry, dead wood that was everywhere around the area. So Sam was also able to fry bacon in a second pan.

"You boys got any coffee?" Gus asked. "I haven't had coffee for days."

"We don't drink it," Tony said, "but I'll look." After searching through the rafting food supplies, he came back with a bag of coffee. Gus had a pot and rainwater that he collected in a barrel.

When the coffee was ready, Gus poured some into his dented aluminum cup and took a drink. "Ahhh!" he said. "That's so good." Then he smacked his lips.

After breakfast Sam said, "The three of us are going down to the river to build the raft. Is it all right if we take Lucky with us?"

"Sure."

"We won't come back to the cabin until after dark."

"That's a good idea. Those buzzards will be keeping watch at least until then. I'll just act like it's a normal day."

"Good. You be careful now," Sam said.

"You boys be careful, too."

"We will."

They loaded an ax, ropes, and the rest of the things they needed for raft building onto Lucky's back, and started off toward the river.

"What if rescuers have been to our camp, saw we were missing, and thought we drowned or something?"

"Quit it, Tyler," Tony threatened. "I mean it."

"Well they could have." He reached in his pocket and took out the gold nugget he'd found earlier, and held it up for Sam and Tony to see. "I can't believe a guy can just dig this stuff out of the ground." The sun made the gold look even more beautiful.

"Wonder how much it's worth?" Tony said.

"Gus told me it's a lot," he said, and smiled.

They climbed down carefully along the jagged, rocky path. Tyler slipped and almost fell. "How we gonna get back up here in the dark?"

"We won't. We'll just climb up at the end of the day and wait till dark. The rest of the path is flat. Remember?"

"I wish I could think of stuff like you do."

"Just work hard. That's what we need right now."

Back at their camp, Sam and his friends took down the tent first. Then they used Lucky to help drag some heavy logs to the river. Next they took turns cutting each log in half with the ax. They worked together to slip logs halfway into the water. Next they tied the logs together with some of Gus' heavy ropes. Sam positioned one rope at each end, and tied a third in the center of the logs.

He had to get into the water to tie the rope at that end. "Man," he said, shaking. "This water is so cold."

After the three ropes were secured, Sam tied long branches in the other direction across the logs and the old flat rubber raft was laid over the branches and tied down with smaller ropes.

Next, the cases with extra food and other supplies were placed at the back of the raft and tied down. They cleaned up their campsite, buried their trash, cleared away the rocks from their fire pit, and covered that, too, until it looked like no one had ever been there.

"Do you really think this raft will make it all the way to Lake Powell?" Tony asked.

"I hope we don't have to find that out," Sam said.

"What do you mean?"

"The way I figure, all we have to do is get away from here. After that I hope somebody sees us."

"Rescuers?" Tyler asked with the first sound of hope in his voice since they'd landed on the riverbank.

"I'd be happy if just another raft full of people spotted us," Sam said. "They'd know right away that a raft like this could never make it the whole way."

Tyler sank back into his usual mood. "Now I'm getting

nervous."

"You're always nervous," Tony teased.

"I mean it. We could get hurt or…"

"There you go again. Always looking at the good stuff."

Sam glanced up at the sky. "We'd better start back. It'll be dark soon." But before they left, he tied a long rope to the back of the raft and attached it to a rock farther up on the beach.

The food case was tied onto Lucky's back and balanced with a few tools and equipment that Sam thought Gus could use in his mine. Then they hurried to the path, carefully climbed the rocks, and waited for Lucky to follow them to the top. They crouched down behind the rocks and bushes at the top of the ridge. In the distance they heard the faint sounds of motorcycles not far from Gus' cabin.

"Look," Tyler said. His voice trailed off to barely a whisper. "Those guys are back."

Sam hoped his plan would work, but how could he know for sure? He swallowed hard, turned to Tyler and said, "I…I know."

CHAPTER 11
SETTING THE TRAPS

Sam and his friends waited until it was completely dark before moving out from their hiding position. In the distance they saw the lights of motorcycles darting across the rocks and trees. The motorcycle riders had built their bikes to make as much noise as possible. And that was only adding to the fear that Sam felt deep inside. He thought about how afraid Gus must have felt out here all alone, before he and his friends had come.

"I hope they don't get any closer," Tyler whispered.

The powerful bikes continued to roar in the distance like a pack of hungry hounds just waiting for the chance to attack.

"Let's try to get back to the cabin," Sam said. "Gus probably wonders if we're okay."

"But what about Lucky?" Tony asked.

Sam looked over to where the donkey stood. "She'll be okay. She lives out here. Those guys see her every day. And Gus probably loads stuff on her all the time. But right now we gotta get inside where it's safe."

They crouched down and slipped through the shadows toward Gus' cabin. A dim, orange light from his lantern spilled out through cracks in the weathered logs of his old place; a cabin that looked like it might fall down any second. Just before Sam and his friends reached the front door, headlights from several motorcycles lined up at the top of the hill overlooking the cabin. Sam and the others also heard that familiar bell as Lucky ambled up behind them.

"Get down," Sam ordered. He motioned with his hand as he continued looking toward the hill. Tony and Tyler ducked out of sight.

"Do you think they might come in here tonight?" Tyler asked.

"How should we know?" Tony said.

Sam and Tony hurried to untie the food case from Lucky's back and it fell to the ground with a thump. Then they inched forward a few more feet. Sam put his hand on the door, gave it a push, and it creaked open as more light from the lantern shined directly on the three boys' faces.

Gus poked his head up from the mineshaft. His shaking hands, wrapped around the handle of a pick-ax, and his wide eyes let Sam know he was terrified. When he saw the boys, he lowered the ax. "Shucks! I'm glad it's only you boys." Then he let out a deep breath he'd been holding.

"Who'd you think it was?" Tyler squeaked.

"You never know back here."

"Did you think it was the claim jumpers?" Tony asked.

The old man nodded. "It could have been."

"How come they don't come in any closer than that hill?" Tyler asked.

"Don't know for sure. I think it's because they don't know if I've struck gold or not yet. Those lazy no goods want me to do all the work and then they can swoop in and get the gold. But it ain't gonna happen that-a-way." He raised his ax a little higher, like a weapon.

"You couldn't fight them off with that thing," Tony said.

"I can try."

"How long do they stay around up there each night?" Sam asked.

"About an hour or so. They make all that noise, and then ride back to their camp."

"You've seen their camp?" Tony asked.

The old man wiped his forehead and nodded.

Sam stepped closer to where Gus stood. "Where is it?"

He pointed off into the distance. "Yonder."

"How far?"

"And you've been there?" Tyler asked.

"I've gone out several nights to see what they're up to. And I kept looking for a way to escape."

"Why didn't you?"

"It's too dangerous on foot, and in the dark." Gus took a deep breath. "I'm not a young man anymore. I couldn't hope to outrun a bunch of guys on motorcycles."

"Would it be hard to get to their camp?" Sam asked.

"You can see their fire from the top of the hill. After they go back to camp, of course."

"Then what do they do?"

"Ride around in the dark, drink, yell, and shoot their pistols."

Tyler could hardly make the words come out. "They've... got...g...guns?"

Just then they heard the sound of shots being fired behind the hill.

"I still don't understand why you haven't tried to find some other way out of here," Tony said.

Now Gus became a little angrier than Sam had seen him since arriving at his claim site. "Can't. There ain't but the one way out of this place. I done told you already. Got the river behind me and only a narrow little pass between me and my truck. They keep the pass guarded. I'm like a prisoner back here. Before you boys come, they were tryin' to starve me out. Almost did, too."

Sam went outside and dragged in the case they had brought with them on Lucky's back. He opened the heavy metal latches, lifted the top, and reached in. Then he pulled out a five-pound bag of sugar. "What time do they go to sleep at night?"

Gus stroked his beard. "Around midnight I think."

A slight smile came to Sam's face. "Then I have one more great idea for them. But it's something I'd never do to anyone unless I was really in trouble, like right now."

"What?" Tyler asked.

"You'll see. Now, here's what we're gonna do tonight." He

went through his entire plan to make sure everyone knew what to do. With the traps already set, all he had left was to sneak into the claim jumpers' camp. He and Tony helped Gus and Tyler dig in the mine for a few hours so the bikers would get tired and go back to their camp.

Sam and his friends found enough gold nuggets to fill a small leather bag Gus kept around his neck. Then, at around midnight, Sam stuck his head outside of the cabin door and listened. "I don't hear them anymore, Tony. You ready to go?"

As usual, Tony did his best to act brave. "I am if you am… I…I mean if you are."

Sam handed his flashlight to Tony and put the bag of sugar under his arm. "Let's go."

The two boys crept out of the cabin, disappeared into the dark, and headed toward the bikers' camp. "Don't forget to watch out for our traps," Sam warned.

"Man, I forgot all about those."

"Good thing those guys don't know about 'em," Sam said.

Sam and Tony would take a few steps, stop, listen, and then move out again. Sam was careful to remember where each trap had been set. Again, a clear sky above and a near full moon gave enough light for them to find their way. But to make sure, they did their best not to walk in the center of the path. Then Sam kept a careful watch for each of the branches that had been tied back, and to avoid any of the trip wires. Finally they made it to the top of the small hill. In the distance raged the evil glow of the claim jumpers' fire.

"It lights up everything around," Tony whispered. "How we gonna get close enough?"

"We just have to, that's all."

By now they had made it safely past the holes, trip tree branches, and stick spikes in the path. "All we gotta do now is listen for rattlesnakes."

Tony grabbed his arm so hard, Sam turned clear around. "What?"

"You didn't say anything about snakes before."

"That's because I knew you wouldn't want to come if I did."

"I didn't want to come anyway. Now I really don't feel good about being out here."

"But you're the guy who's always doing the dangerous stuff."

"I know, but I can't *stand* snakes."

"A big guy like you?"

"I don't care if I'm ten feet tall, a snake is a snake."

"Just listen for them. Those snakes'll let us know if we come too close."

"They won't have to. I'll be back in the cabin before they can open one eye."

Sam motioned forward. "Come on."

Rocks and bushes continued to give them places to hide as they came closer and closer to the camp. Sam's throat turned as dry as the dead brush he crept through. So far there had been no snakes. At least he didn't think so. The bikers' fire made it easy to see where each man slept on the ground, and if that wasn't enough, the sounds of their snoring did the rest. Each of them sprawled out on a sleeping bag with their feet pointed toward the warm fire.

After Sam had moved as close as possible, he crouched down. "It's too dangerous to walk any closer. We need to crawl from now on."

"Crawl where?"

He rose up over a big rock and pointed. "See their bikes over there?"

Tony looked where his friend pointed. "So?"

"They're making our job too easy."

"What job? I thought we were just coming to have a look?"

Sam shook his head. "Why in the world would I drag a five pound bag of sugar around with me out here if I only wanted a look?"

"I thought that was strange, but you said you had a plan."

"That I do. They lined their motorcycles up all in one place. This is like one of those old westerns where the good guys come in and take the horses from the bad guys so they've got nothing to ride on and can't chase the good guys."

"You watch too many movies."

"Maybe so, but this time those movies gave me the idea."

"What idea? You think the two of us can sneak into their camp, ride all their motorcycles away, and nobody's gonna hear the roar of the bikes? Plus…we don't know anything about riding one of those things in the first place."

Sam smiled. "Think of them as jet skis...but on land."

Tony answered almost loud enough to wake the bikers. “Are you serious?”

Sam put a finger to his lips, shook his head, and whispered, “We aren’t gonna ride their bikes.”

Tony let out a deep breath. “That’s a relief. But I still think they’re gonna be too heavy for us to push, and even if we did… one noise and those guys’d grab us for sure.”

Sam shook his head again and whispered. “Not gonna push ’em either.”

“What, then?”

Sam held up the bag of sugar. “This.”

“You gonna dump it on them while they’re sleeping so ants come and bite ’em?”

“That’s not a bad idea. I saw that in a movie, too, only they used honey. But I got something much, much better.”

Tony looked over toward the bikes again. “I still don’t get it.”

“Come on. You will.”

CHAPTER 12
INTO THE BIKERS' CAMP

Sam and Tony crouched down and moved to their right, in a half circle, until they were only a few feet away from eight dirty, dented motorcycles. If anyone saw that he and Tony were there, Sam knew something terrible would happen. Then he dropped down flat on the ground. He took one more look around the area, and then began crawling in the dirt toward the bikes. With one hand he pushed the bag of sugar ahead of him, crawled forward, and pushed it again.

One of the men suddenly snorted and sat up. He seemed to look around, grunted, scratched his stomach, then slumped back down and began snoring again.

Sam gulped, took a deep breath, and whispered to Tony, "I can't believe there aren't any guards." Then he started pushing the bag of sugar again. *Sure hope I don't poke a hole in it*, he thought as he crawled on the ground like a lizard. Finally he and

Tony reached a large tree. They hid there for a few minutes, right next to the first motorcycle.

"Now what?" Tony asked.

"Your job will be to open the gas caps. Then I'll dump sugar in each tank. After that you just close them up again."

"WHAT?" Tony said out loud.

Sam covered his friend's mouth. "Quiet," he whispered.

The dust from Sam's hand nearly made Tony sneeze. "What's the sugar for?"

"After they fire up their bikes tomorrow, it'll go down the gas lines. When it hits that hot engine…look out."

"Now I get it. Like in my science class last year when Mr. Tanner heated up some sugar in a test tube."

Sam smiled and nodded.

"But what's it gonna do to the bikes?"

"They'll just quit running, that's what."

"And these bikers will hafta take them someplace to be fixed?"

Sam nodded.

"Boy, those guys are really gonna be mad."

Sam continued nodding. "Yes they are." He motioned for them to move forward. "Let's go."

They eased around from behind the tree and knelt next to the first bike. Tony twisted open the gas cap while Sam tore the paper at the top of the bag. After he dumped sugar in the tank, Tony closed the cap. Then they moved on to the next bike and did the same thing. On and on they worked in the dark until they reached the last one. Tony had a hard time getting the cap on that bike to budge. When it finally did come loose, he was turning the cap so hard, it flew up out of his hand and when it came down, before he could catch it, the cap struck the gas tank on the next bike. It wouldn't have been so bad on a full tank, but when a metal tank like that one was only half full, it sounded more like a drum. So, when the cap glanced off of it, the tank sounded like someone had hit a big gong.

Sam and Tony dropped to the ground like dead men as several of the bikers grunted and moved around in their sleep. For a few moments, Sam was certain his heart had stopped beating. When he was sure no one was coming toward them, he got back up on his knees and poured the rest of his sugar into the last tank.

Tony felt around in the dirt until he found the cap, put it back on the tank, and both began crawling away.

Before Sam and Tony made it back to the safety of the bushes, a booming voice demanded, "What's going on here?"

Every man in the camp jumped to his feet. At first they acted confused, almost as if they weren't awake yet. Sam and Tony stopped dead still; sure they'd just been caught. Tony even raised his arms into the air. They slowly turned around, and when they did, they saw the biggest, meanest-looking man in the gang standing near the fire.

"What's wrong?" one of the others mumbled in a half-stupid voice.

"Look at you slobs. You're all asleep. No one's standing guard. What if somebody tried to sneak in the camp? Would anyone notice?"

Sam and Tony smiled and almost laughed.

"Nobody's never come back here 'cept us," one of the others argued.

"But what if they did? Now, one of you guys get your lazy bones up and guard the camp." The man closest to the fire slipped out of his sleeping bag, pulled on his dirty, black leather boots, stood up, and shuffled up to a high point overlooking the camp.

One of the other men sat up in his bed, rubbed his eyes, yawned, and stretched. "Wh…what are you doing here, boss?"

"Me and the boys think that old coot down there has struck his gold. We're gonna let him work till noon tomorrow. Then we're goin' in."

Sam's chest quickly tightened. He nearly choked, making it hard to breathe for a moment. Then he managed to whisper, "We gotta get back."

He and Tony snuck out to the safety of the rocks and bushes. From there they stood up and hurried to the main path. Suddenly they heard something that caused both boys to stiffen as they stood perfectly still.

Without even moving his mouth Tony asked through his teeth, "Is that what I think it is?"

Sam nodded. "Uh huh."

"Where is he?"

"Right in front of us."

"What'll we do?"

"Give me the flashlight."

"You crazy? We turn that thing on and all those guys will see us for sure."

"It's them or that rattler. Either way, it's all over."

Tony groaned. "Great choice."

"Besides," Sam said, "I don't think they'll see us. I just need a couple short bursts from the light so we can see where the thing is."

Tony handed the light to Sam. Tony's hand shook so hard, Sam nearly dropped the flashlight. He switched it on while holding his fingers over the front. Only a little light spilled out, but it was enough to show them exactly where Mr. Fang was sitting…and rattling. Sam and Tony slowly crept around him, in an extra wide circle, then hurried away.

As big as Tony was, his voice still quivered. "I really hate those things. Especially at night."

"Yeah, but isn't it cool the way they let you know where they are?"

"Yeah…cool," Tony said in a nervous laugh.

"Really. Think if they didn't make a sound, like cobras. Those guys just stand right up out of the grass, flatten that head of theirs, and bam! You'd be walking around out here, step on one of them, and wham-o!"

"I still don't like 'em," Tony said.

When they came to the area where the traps had been hidden earlier, they picked their way carefully through the minefield of biker hazards they'd set. "I'm glad none of these make any noise," Tony said. Then he grinned. "Those guys won't know what hit 'em."

Because Sam and Tony were being extra careful, it took a long time to return to Gus' mining camp. When they stepped back into the cabin, they found Gus and Tyler still digging in the mine.

"We've got a problem," Sam told them.

Both diggers jumped at the sound of Sam's voice. "You scared us!" Tyler grabbed his chest and tried to catch his breath.

They stopped digging and sat on wooden boxes to rest. Gus took a rag out of his pocket and wiped sweat from his face, neck, and hands. "And what's the problem?" he asked.

"We heard them talking in their camp."

"Those men should have been asleep long ago," Gus said.

Tony cleared his throat. "They were, but then this great big guy came in and woke them all up."

"Was he wearing black leather?" Gus asked.

Tony looked to Sam and nodded. Then he turned back to Gus. "I think so. It was dark."

"But he was a big man?"

"Real big."

"And he has a shiny, bald head?"

Both boys nodded.

Gus looked down and shook his head. "This is not good. Not good at all. People can be very dangerous when they get greedy."

"What's wrong?" Tyler asked.

"Tony and I heard them talking about coming down here at

noon."

Gus's eyes widened. "Tomorrow?"

"It's tomorrow already," Tyler said, tapping a finger on his watch.

"Today," Tony said.

"Whadda ya think we should do?" Sam asked.

"We already have plenty of gold to prove I have a gold mine," Gus said. "And we know there's no way we can make it to my truck."

Tyler sat up a little straighter. "So what's that leave us?"

Sam turned and looked toward the river.

"Oh no you don't," Tyler complained. "There's no way you're gettin' me out on that river with a dumpy raft. You never said anything about actually *using* it. Probably fall apart when we hit the first rapids."

Gus held up his hands. "Listen. Those guys out there aren't playing around. They've got guns and they mean to stop us."

Tyler shrugged his shoulders. "So what are we s'pos'ta do about it?"

"They said noon," Sam said. "That means we got the whole morning. You and Gus have to get down to the raft before us. I showed you how Lucky has to help push the raft into the river. Then you leave the long rope tied the way I have it around the rock. When we come, and trust me, we'll be running as fast as we can, you guys be ready to shove off."

"We?" Tony asked.

Sam looked to him.

"You said when *we* come running."

"You and I have to be the ones to lead those guys into our traps."

"Now I don't feel so good," Tyler cried.

Tony turned to him. "What's your problem? You'll already be safe on the raft."

"Safe? On the raft? That's a good one."

"Stop it, both of you," Sam scolded. "If we have any hope of getting away from those guys, we all gotta work together."

"This is one morning I wish would never come," Tyler sighed.

Sam folded his arms. "Well, it's comin'."

CHAPTER 13
HERE THEY COME

Sam turned to Gus. “Do you have any dynamite?”

“*Dynamite*?” Tyler cried. He started shaking all over. That made his voice shake, too, and his eyes blinked. “Now I know we’re gonna die.”

Gus gave Sam a quizzical look. “I have a few sticks, but they’re very dangerous.”

“I don’t want the dynamite, just the fuses.”

“Got plenty of those.”

“Do you have any tape?”

Gus reached up onto a high shelf. “How about this black electrical tape?”

“Perfect. Matches?”

“Over by the stove.”

“What are you planning?” Tony asked.

“A little diversion. I just want them to think it’s real.” He went back outside and found a broken wooden ladder with round rungs about the same size as a stick of dynamite. They were too long so with a small saw Gus kept next to the stove, he cut the ladder parts into shorter pieces. Next he cut fuses about two feet long. After those were ready, Sam wrapped the black tape around three sticks at a time. He jammed a fuse into the middle and taped it.

Doubtful, Tyler said, “Those don’t look very real.”

Sam quickly lit one of the fuses and tossed the fake dynamite at his friend’s feet. Tyler leaped out of the way, hid behind the bed, and covered his ears. “What are you tryin’ to do? Kill me?”

“Just wanted to show you that if something gets tossed at you like that, and the fuse is burning, a person isn’t going to stop and notice much more. The first thing he’ll do is run, just like you did.”

Tony laughed. “Yeah.” He crossed his arms and put one hand to his chin. “Not too many people are gonna stand there and say, ‘You know, Bob, that doesn’t look like real dynamite to me. It looks more like parts from an old wood ladder taped together.’” Then he laughed even harder.

“And that’s what I’m counting on,” Sam said. “They’ll think it’s real all right.” He finished making four bundles of fake dynamite and stuffed those into his backpack.

A few minutes later Tony came and sat down where Sam worked. “I’m a little worried about something.”

“Why? Have you been around Tyler too long?”

“What if our raft does come apart in the rapids? We’d never

make it against that river. And the water is way colder than the ocean back home."

Sam took a deep breath. "I know. That's why we only need it to get away. After that we can go back on the riverbank and try to flag down some other rafters."

"That makes me feel a lot better. I thought you might try to take it through the really bad stuff."

Sam shook his head as he smoothed down the electrical tape on another bundle of fake dynamite. "Not if I can help it."

Later, everyone worked a little longer in the mine. They dug out the rocks with their shovels so Gus could break them apart with his pickax.

After work, they slept for a few hours then gathered inside Gus's cabin for a late breakfast.

"I wish you boys coulda come here a long time ago. With the four of us working this mine, we might be done by now."

"How'd those guys find out about your mine?" Tony asked.

Gus spit on the ground. "Oh, it was so stupid of me. I'd been careful, real careful."

"What happened?" Tyler asked.

"After I first discovered the mine, I built my cabin to hide everything. Even had some rafters come up in here from the river one day, like you boys did, but they never suspected a thing."

"So what went wrong?" Sam asked.

"I went into town one afternoon in my old truck. Even then I covered the hole up so's nobody'd know it was there. I ran into an old friend on the street. When he asked me what I was doing nowadays I sorta, kinda, mighta said the word…gold."

"Then what?" Tony asked.

"These two men were standing next to their motorcycles about as close as you boys are to me right now."

"And they heard you?"

The old man nodded his head, then shook it. "Stupid, stupid, stupid!"

"We have more important things to worry about right now," Sam said.

Tyler smiled. "See. You're finally starting to think like I do."

"I'll never go that far. But everything has to work perfectly. It wouldn't hurt to pray about it while you're getting ready." Then Sam glanced at his watch. "Eleven. Time to get moving. You all know what to do."

Tyler pointed to his chest. "We do?"

Sam glared back at him.

He looked down with a silly grin. "Oh, yeah. Guess we do."

Gus, Tyler, and Lucky began making their way toward the river.

"Remember," Sam told them, "that raft has to be ready to go as soon as me and Tony hit the beach. If it isn't, the whole plan falls apart."

"If that happens," Tyler said, "we're sunk."

"Don't say things like that," Tony scolded.

"We'll be ready," Gus said. "I used to know a trick or two about this river.

"Good. Let's get started." Sam grabbed his backpack.

Tony followed him toward the hill. "Exactly what are we supposed to do up there?"

"Confuse them, see if the sugar stops their bikes, knock down most of them, and then run like thunder to the river."

Tony's voice went up higher. "That's *all*?"

"It's enough."

"Yer tellin' me."

Like before, Sam and Tony picked their way carefully through the traps in the dirt and the others in the trees. One wrong step and the trick would be on them. At the top of the hill, Sam motioned for them to stop. He took out his binoculars and focused on the camp. Moving from left to right, he searched the entire area. Then he began looking back toward the left.

Suddenly he stopped.

Trembling, Tony asked, "What is it?"

Sam swallowed hard. "They're comin'. Get down."

Immediately they dropped to their knees. Sam began sweating all over. Right then the sun seemed a hundred degrees hotter than before. His mouth went dry. His throat started burning. He fumbled around to take off his backpack and his voice went hoarse. "Could you help me with this?"

Tony slipped the pack off of Sam's shoulders. "Are you sure you know what we're doing?"

"Hope so."

"You *hope*?"

"Listen. I want you to go back to the other end of the traps and wait for me."

"And what will you be doing?"

Sam smiled slightly. "Confusion, remember?"

"Then what do I do?"

"When they get to the top of the hill and look down, I want you to start jumping around and yelling, "*Gold*! We found *gold*!"

"But I thought we weren't supposed to tell."

"Just do it. You heard them last night. They already know anyway."

Tony began taking shorter breaths. "Then what?"

"I think they'll try to run from my dynamite, and when they do, our traps should wipe them all out."

"They'd better."

Sam peered through the binoculars again. "Here they come. Hurry, we don't have much time."

Tony moved as fast as he could down the path and Sam hurried toward the bikers. Right then, he felt a little like David in the Bible, with a whole pack of Goliaths storming straight toward him. When he found a good hiding spot behind the rocks, he stopped and waited. The thundering sounds of roaring motorcycles came closer. As they did, Sam's heart only pounded harder and faster. His hands shook and he wondered if he'd be able to strike the matches. Even then he thought he might shake the fuses right out of the stick bundles. He turned to check on Tony who was already in position.

The roar from the approaching bikes became deafening, then suddenly it died down. Sam lifted his head up just high enough so he could see what was happening. The first thing he saw was that one of the bikes had stopped. Smoke poured out of its exhaust like the smokestack on Gus' potbellied stove back at the cabin. Several of the other riders had also stopped to see what was wrong. Then the same thing happened to a second bike, and a third. Soon smoke nearly covered the entire area where the bikes had come to a stop.

The biggest man, the one Sam had seen the night before, brought his menacing motorcycle around to the other stalled machines. He removed the cap from one of the gas tanks, pulled off a black, leather glove, and touched his finger just inside the opening. Sam watched as he pressed his fingers together several quick times. Then he wiped the fingers on his vest. After that, he turned and looked toward Gus' cabin. He slammed a fist into his hand several times, then pounded the handlebars, but never stopped looking off in the direction of the cabin. Next he started beating on his chest and growled like a bear. Then Sam heard him say, "Leave your busted bikes here. We'll get that old buzzard!"

The three men dropped their bikes in the dirt and headed toward Sam's hiding place behind the rock.

CHAPTER 14
DESPERATE ESCAPE

I sure hope Gus and Tyler are ready, Sam thought with a gulp. He looked out to see the other four men still riding their motorcycles. Then he wondered if he'd missed any with the sugar. *Too late to think about that now.* He took one of the long, wooden, stick matches Gus had given him, and got ready to strike it on a rock beside his head. By now the men's voices were getting louder, which could only mean they were dangerously close. Sam turned and gave Tony a hand signal.

Tony rushed out of the bushes, started jumping around, and waving his arms in the air like a wild man. "Gold!" he yelled at the top of his voice. "We found gold! Its gold I tell ya!"

Even Sam was convinced. He poked his head out just long enough to see the big man in black leather ride his bike up to the edge of the hill first. When he stopped, he motioned for the other men to be quiet and to turn off their bikes. Then he, along with Sam and all the others, heard very clearly at the bottom of the hill, "Gold! Lots and lots of gold!" Tony continued jumping around as he yelled. He'd lean down, pick up handfuls of dirt, throw them into the air, and dance around some more.

"Hey, boss," one of the men said. "You was right. There *is* gold down there."

"Well of course there is. But where did that kid come from?"

"I don't know, boss. We been watching that pass every minute."

The big man put his hands on his hips and spun around. "You mean like last night when I caught all of you sorry slugs sleeping?"

The other man looked down. "That was different."

"How? Tell me. How was it different?"

"Because…nobody's gonna come back here at night. Only an idiot would…do…"

The big man growled and became even angrier than before. "I came back here last night."

"Yeah, boss, but I meant no dumb kid would do that."

The large man turned back around and looked down at Tony. "There must be more of them around here. That old coot brought them in somehow."

One of the other men started looking around. Then he raised his hand.

"This ain't school, Melvin," another biker said.

"Uh huh. But I don't think there's no more kids."

"Gold! We're rich!" Tony continued yelling as he did a little dirt dance.

Sam lit the fuses to all four of his fake dynamite bundles. Then he stood straight up next to the rock where he'd been hiding. He leaned against the rock a little for two reasons. He hoped the men wouldn't see him shaking, and he didn't want to pass out and fall down. With a serious voice he said, "Yes, there *are* more kids."

"Um." A man on one of the motorcycles asked, "What's that you got in your hands there?"

"Can't you see, you big dummy?" the large man thundered. "It's *dynamite*. Hit the dirt!"

All the men dove for cover as Sam threw the bundles, one by one, so smoke from their fuses rose into the air in several places. Then he waited.

Melvin rose up first. His face was completely covered with dirt. All Sam could see were his eyes and his mouth. "How come these things ain't going off?" he asked.

"Count your lucky stars, you idiot," another biker said.

Then Melvin crawled forward and picked up one of the bundles. The fuse continued burning. He stood up and took it over to the big man. "I got somethin' for ya boss."

The boss uncovered his ears and looked at Melvin. "Throw that thing away or you ain't gonna believe the somethin' I got for you."

Melvin reached over and pulled the fuse out. "Look, boss. The dumb thing ain't real."

"Are we talking about the dynamite, or you, Melvin?"

Melvin held up the sticks. "See?"

The big man's face became bright red. Veins even stuck out on his shaved head. He glared back at Sam and motioned for the others to charge. "Get him!" The men on foot began running toward Sam.

Sam looked toward Tony for an instant, then back to the men, and said quickly, "Gotta-go."

Sam heard the other riders fire up their bikes and roar off toward the path. He carefully made his way down through the traps. As he ran he yelled, "Run, Tony. Run!"

But because he was still yelling at the top of his voice, Tony didn't seem to hear him. "Gold! We've got lots and lots of gold!" Tony said. Then he laughed wildly like a sun-crazed prospector. By now he wasn't dancing around nearly as fast as before and sweat poured from his face.

Sam looked over his shoulder as the front tire of the first motorcycle that was still running hit one of the sharp sticks he had placed in the path. He heard a sudden pop, followed by a hissing sound. The rider stopped his bike, looked down at the flattening tire and said, "Of all the luck." He jumped off and pushed his bike off the path. Just then a second bike hit another of the sticks. His front tire also exploded. Then a third bike began belching smoke from the sugar, just like all of the others.

Sam clenched his fists. "It's working," He continued moving away while the men hurried on foot down the path after him. Big mistake for them!

The first man tripped one of the ropes and a tree branch flew out of nowhere. It caught him right in the chest and threw him clear off the path into the bushes.

"Run, Tony. Run!"

Three of the other men fell into hidden holes covered with branches and dirt. As Sam looked back, tree branches got most of the others until one of the last men fell into the very last hole. But when Sam looked again, the boss had grabbed the only motorcycle that still worked. He could hear the man trying to start it.

When Sam rushed down to where Tony was, he didn't even stop as he shot right past. Over his shoulder he screamed, "Run for your life!"

"But what about the gold?"

"That part's over. Now *get out of here*."

Tony caught up to him as they ran to the rocky path that led down to the river, the raft, and safety…Sam hoped. As they hurried about half way down the rocks, the big man roared to the top of that hill and stopped. He glared at them while he throttled his motor, and got ready to roar down the path to get them.

Tony huffed and puffed behind Sam. "No way he can ride that thing down here. Right?"

"Just keep moving. Hurry." Sam looked back again to see that the man had gotten off his bike and now ran toward them almost as fast as they were trying to get away. He also noticed that some of the other men must have gotten out of the holes and joined their boss in the chase.

Sam reached the flat ground first and ran toward the raft.

"Shove off!" he cried out to Gus and Tyler. Then he watched helplessly as they tried to move the heavy log raft into the water.

Tyler cried back in terror, "It won't budge!"

"Lucky. Remember Lucky," Sam called out.

Tyler snapped his fingers. "Right." He began using Lucky's strength to help move the heavy raft.

Just then the big man tripped and did a somersault, landing in the dirt on flat ground. That gave Sam the extra seconds he needed to get to the rock and untie his rope. But when he looked back, the giant was back on his feet and running faster than ever, sweat dripping from his face and bald head.

Tony reached Gus and Tyler first. And it was a good thing he did because, with his size and strength, he helped them push for the last few feet until the entire log raft sat in the water. Sam grabbed the rope from around the rock and began running for the raft.

The other three yelled, "Come on, Sam. You can make it. Run!" By now, some of the other bikers had also reached the flat ground and, together with their boss, they raced toward the river's edge.

Like a fullback sprinting toward the goal line, Sam barely held onto the end of the rope as he strained to get to the raft while the boss and the others raced toward him. Sam flung his rope into the air, thinking it would sail out and land on the raft, but it didn't. It went over his head and landed on the ground behind him…right in front of the first man who was chasing him.

The raft slowly pulled away from the bank. Sam reached the edge of the beach and with one last push, leaped across the water and landed in the middle of the raft where the others grabbed him. Gasping for air, he said, "Whew. That was a close one." Gus and Tony used long poles to push farther away from the riverbank. Their heavy raft began picking up speed in the water. "I never thought you'd make it." Tyler said.

"It looked like they were going to get you," Gus grunted while pushing on his pole as hard as he could.

But before he could say a word, Sam turned back toward the riverbank, saw something that scared him worse than anything he'd seen so far on the whole trip, and groaned, "Oh no."

CHAPTER 15
DANGEROUS WOODEN RAFT

Even though their raft was already at a safe distance away from the riverbank, part of the long, long rope Sam had used to tie it to a rock was still on the beach. Like a snake, slowly slithering in the hot sun, the rope now dragged across the sand near the water.

Sam and the others stared in terror as the motorcycle gang's boss rushed toward the rope. He tripped and fell in the soft sand, but was able to crawl the rest of the way.

Then everything seemed to switch into slow motion in Sam's mind as the man on the beach got up, leaped, and flew through the air toward the end of that rope, as if he were making an Olympic style dive into water. Sam scrambled to the back of the raft, dropped to his knees, and thrust his hand into the water. He fumbled around until he found his end of the rope and pulled on it as hard as he could. He looked up to see the other end jump forward, just in time, causing the man to miss it by what looked like less than an inch. As the boss hit the dirt and thrust his hands out to grasp the rope, he came up with nothing more than two hands full of beach sand.

Everyone on the raft cheered and began jumping around.

"Stop it," Sam warned. "We don't want this thing to break apart."

"We're finally safe," Tyler said. Then he put his fingers in his ears, stuck his tongue out and made funny noises. "Naa naa naa boo boo, we got away from you."

The rafters looked back to see the motorcycle gang lining the riverbank with their fists in the air. "Well get you for this," one of them threatened. His frightening voice echoed out over the smooth water.

Sam pulled the rest of the long rope in and coiled it at the back of the raft. He reminded the others to tie ropes around their waists for safety. After they did that, he and Tyler also grabbed one of the long poles Sam and Tony had left on the deck of the raft. They used those to push themselves farther away from danger as quickly as possible.

Soon their raft drifted out of the calm water near where they had been camped and into the swift current of the Colorado River again. After his heart rate had settled a bit, Sam said, "Who's hungry?"

"Who isn't?" Tony answered. He set his long pole down on the deck.

"I wonder if we'll see any other rafts today?" Tyler asked.

"There are a lot of them this time of year," Gus told them.

Sam opened the food cases and passed around water, crackers, cookies, biscuits, jam, and apples. For a little while, it felt more like just another lazy afternoon at a picnic.

"What's gonna happen to Lucky?" Tyler asked.

"Well sir," Gus said, "I found her in the wild and she'll probably die in the wild."

Tyler's voice trembled. "She's gonna die?"

"No. No. Lucky'll be all right for now. I 'spect she'll just wander around those hills till I get back."

"When will that be?" Tony asked.

"After we get to Moab…if we ever *get* to Moab."

"We'll get there," Sam told them.

Tony turned to Gus. "You got any kids or anything?"

"No sir, I don't. Had a wife once, though."

"What happened to her?"

"She just plumb wore out before I did, I guess."

"Was that before you started living way out here?"

"It was the reason for it. I've never knowed another one like her. We had such big plans. I guess that's why you should enjoy the life you have right here, right now, 'cause you never know what's around the next bend in the river."

As soon as Gus said that, all three boys sat a little straighter and turned their eyes and ears toward the front of the raft.

"What's that?" Tyler asked. Cracker pieces dropped from his wide-open mouth.

Gus shook his head. "That, my friends, is the reason I told

you we couldn't leave my camp by traveling on this river."

With his mouth full, Tony said, "Sounds like a freight train."

Gus nodded. "Might as well be."

Sam stuffed the last piece of biscuit into his mouth and then muffled, "Get your poles." By this time, the raft had already begun to pick up speed, racing straight toward that roar.

"Probably one of the category fours I read about," Tony yelled.

"Tighten your ropes." Sam cautioned as he made sure his was tight, too. Without warning, their raft hit a whirlpool that spun them completely around. "Try to turn it back," he shouted.

The brave rafters, along with Gus, struggled against the mighty flow of the Colorado and nearly had the raft going in the right direction again when Tyler's pole got caught between two rocks. Even though he tried his best to hold on, the pole snapped off in the powerful current. "How come that always happens to me?"

"Just grab another one from under our old rubber raft. I made plenty," Sam said. "If we ever hit one of the rapids going sideways, this thing will fly apart in a zillion pieces."

Sam noticed that Gus did the best job of steering and asked, "How'd you learn how to do that?"

"Do what?"

"Aim the raft like you do."

"I haven't always been a prospector, ya know."

Tyler looked over to him. "Now I feel a lot better."

"Well you shouldn't."

"Because?"

"Because I quit leading rafters after I had a really bad accident on the river."

"Hey," Tony said. "I know who you are now. I read about that. I saw where you lost six people on one of your trips."

"It's true," the old man said, "but it was their own fault."

"What happened?" Sam asked.

"The rain had been falling for a few days. We were camped out along the river, waiting for a storm to pass, but it just kept pounding the area. I was going to call for rescue to come in and haul us out but this one raft full of hotdogs wanted to take the trip anyway. I tried to get 'em to wait but it was no use. They shoved off before I could do anything."

"Then what?" Sam asked.

"With big rains come big rapids. I've never seen them so dangerous as they were that day. That raft of theirs didn't have a chance. A rescue party found it down river a few days later, lookin' like it'd gone through a shredder."

"And the people?"

"Never found 'em. And I never did know how anybody could prove if they died or not. After that, I went to jail. There was a trial, only I wasn't found guilty for their deaths."

"Why not?" Tyler asked.

"The others on the trip testified that I did everything I could. Still, my license was taken away. They really didn't need to do that. After what happened, I never wanted to be on the river again for the rest of my life."

"But you're on it now," Tyler said.

"All I can say is you boys better get ready for the ride of your life. And if we make it through this part, it only gets worse."

Tyler gulped. He reached down and gave his safety rope an extra tug.

Their raft sailed over some larger waves in the river. Sam got a funny feeling in his stomach like when his father drove the car over a dip in a country road. When the car came from the bottom of the dip, Sam remembered how it made his stomach do a small flip-flop. Now it was happening again each time the raft dove down and then rose up on the next wave.

"No matter what happens," Sam reminded his friends, "God is watching. He knows where we are, He knows where we're going, and He knows exactly what's gonna happen to us."

"Wish He'd tell us," Tyler complained.

"Sometimes it's better not to know," Gus told them.

Everyone grabbed onto the poles a little tighter, trying to keep the helpless raft going in the right direction. They passed through a few more of those stomach-flipping waves and then the raft glided out into smoother water. It kept moving fast, but there weren't any big waves.

"Gus," Sam asked. "Do you believe in God?"

"Sure do. I wouldn't start out a day without Him."

"Really?" Tony asked. "We all go to the same church."

"Splendid," he said.

"I hope everybody on this raft's going where they're supposed to right now," Tyler said.

"What on earth are you talking about?" Tony asked.

"Oh, I don't know. I just thought if there was anybody like Jonah or something."

Tony let out a deep breath. "You mean you'd throw him into the river so everyone else would be safe?"

Tyler nodded. "Kinda."

Tony opened his mouth to say something else, but he and the others heard one of those river freight trains again in the distance.

Sam searched the river out in front of them. Then he called out in terror, "Category four…dead ahead!"

CHAPTER 16
KILLER RAPIDS

Sam gripped his wooden pole twice as hard as before. His legs tensed and his back began to hurt from the sudden strain. He felt his knees lock in position and his breathing get faster. With his eyes wide open he said, "Lord...please help us."

The first rapids thundered only a few yards in front of their raft. Sam took one more look around, tightened his safety rope, and prepared for the worst. *Can't believe were in trouble with angry water again*, he thought, remembering the storm that had landed them on Lost Island back home. He looked around to make sure Tony, Tyler, and Gus held their poles ready to push away from any dangerous rocks they were sure to pass.

When he turned back around, Sam almost couldn't believe what he saw. Water from the river seemed to strike rocks and shoot straight up into the air. He used to like the log flume rides at water parks because he always knew that they ended safely.

Oh, the riders might get a little wet, but there was never any real danger. Except this was different. He and the others were in a life and death ride right now.

"Steer to the left!" Gus called from the back of the raft. They fought against the powerful current with all their might, but it seemed silly.

"It's no use," Tyler cried out.

Their helpless raft continued streaking straight toward the rocks. "Left, I tell you. Left!" Gus commanded

The end of Sam's pole found a rock under the surface of the water. He gave just enough of a push to the front of their raft that it turned slightly to the left. A fallen log raced past them on the right. They all stopped and watched as the current drove it out of sight under a large, submerged boulder. The powerful water caught the log's back end, threw it into the air, and the log, as big around as a full-grown tree, snapped off like a twig.

Sam heard the snap as their raft passed by only inches from the dangerous rocks. It reminded him of the sound they heard when the mast from their catamaran snapped from the wind on their way to Lost Island. Sam turned his attention from the broken log back to the dangers right in front of them. In terror he shouted, "Sideways…we're going sideways!"

"It's all right," Gus yelled back. "It's wide enough here."

They shot through rocks on both sides with only inches to spare at the front and back of the raft. When the river spit them out on the other end of the rapid, Gus guided, "Straighten her out now. The next one's narrow."

Sam turned to Gus. "Good thing you used to do this as a guide."

The old man smiled back at him.

With Gus taking more control of the raft, Sam tried to relax a little, but he still couldn't. Racing through raging waters, the battered crew had only seconds to get turned in the right direction again using their poles.

"I really hate this," Tyler shouted.

"We're just gettin' started," Gus told them.

The crew did the best they could to stay balanced on their knees while that ragged raft dipped up and down in the current like a wild, bucking horse that hadn't yet been broken, and Sam could see that this was one river they could never tame. He looked ahead of the raft, and saw the boiling water from the next rapids. He turned back to the others. "Here she comes."

At first the front end of the raft dipped slightly in the water. Immediately it shot nearly straight up in the air. Down it slammed again against the water only to go flying high up again. Then, without warning, they struck something hidden under the water.

Everyone except Tyler lost their balance and tumbled to the deck. But he was crouched down on the exact spot where the raft hit whatever was under the water. As Sam fell onto the deck, backwards, he turned his head just in time to see Tyler go sailing straight up into the air like he'd been on a trampoline. When he came down again, there was no raft under him. Instead, he landed in the frigid water, went under for a moment, and then began bobbing up and down like a beach ball behind the raft.

"Somebody get his rope," Sam called out. Tony and Gus scrambled across the bumpy deck, grabbed Tyler's rope and frantically pulled him toward them.

"Hurry," Sam cried. "More rapids…dead ahead!" He had no time to watch what the others were doing. All he could do was try to steer their raft through the next water roller coaster. This part of the river roared louder than any of the other rapids before. Whitewater swirled around on all sides, while a giant wave rolled only a few feet from the raft. "It's gonna be a bad one!" he shouted at the top of his voice.

This time, instead of dipping first, the front of their raft streaked into the air. Sam quickly looked to the back as Tyler crawled up onto the deck. His thin body shook all over from the cold water.

"Nice going," Sam called out to the others. "You okay, Tyler?"

His friend didn't answer. Sam was proud of him for grabbing another pole right away to help Gus and Tony prepare to do battle with the river again.

About a minute later, the strangest thing happened. As the river widened again, Sam and his friends continued battling against the waves and violent current. Then a large rubber raft, filled with people from another rafting group, raced right past them.

Tyler was the first to yell, "Help. Somebody help us… *please!*"

Then they all joined in. Everyone, including Gus, waved

their arms and screamed for help, but the river roared so loudly the other rafters didn't seem to hear them. They simply smiled and waved as their raft shot past. One of them even snapped a picture of Sam and his raft of doom. As seconds ticked by, the river grew steadily louder with category five rapids now straight ahead!

Even though they were still in calmer waters between rapids, one of the main ropes holding the log raft together suddenly came loose. Two logs on the right side separated from the raft and drifted away. "It's comin' apart," Tyler screamed as he quickly jumped off of a third log just as it broke away.

"Make sure the rest of the ropes are tight," Sam told them. He knelt down to check the one at the front end.

Gus called up to Sam. "We have to get off this here river, son. I don't think this raft of yours can hold together much longer."

"How?"

"We got one more bad stretch to get through. If we make it, there might be a chance."

"*If* we make it?" Tyler screeched.

"We have to!" Tony said.

Sam took a quick look to see that the rest were ready. "Then everybody, check your ropes. Make sure your life jackets are tight, too. Tyler, you okay?"

"I guess so. Thanks for pulling me back in, you guys."

"Do you think those people knew we're in trouble?" Tony asked.

"We can only hope. Now get ready." Sam sank to his knees

so he could rest up for the next rapids. His friends did the same. Then he noticed that Gus had started working on something at the back of the raft. "What are you doing, Gus?"

Without looking up he said, "Makin' a rudder."

"What for?" Tyler asked.

"Might help us steer her a little better…I hope."

"Great idea, Gus. But hurry, will ya?" Sam said.

"I'm going as fast as I can. This raft ain't exactly sittin' still, ya know." He continued tying ropes close together between the center logs that were still connected on the raft. Finally he slipped two long poles into the rope slot he'd made.

Sam stood again. "Let's test it out." He watched as the old man pushed the poles to one side. When he did, the raft turned slightly.

"Gus," Tony said. "You're a genius."

"True, but I'm an *old* genius. One of you boys is gonna have to help me hold onto this thing."

"Why don't all three of you do it?" Sam said. "Our poles aren't much good anyway."

"What are you gonna to do?" Tyler asked.

"I'll stay up here as a look out, and tell you which way to turn."

"Good idea," Tony said.

Tyler started laughing almost uncontrollably.

"What's so funny?" Tony asked.

Through gasps for breath he said, "I just…thought it was f…funny when he said l…look out." Then he threw his head back, looked toward the sky, and sounding more like the coyotes they'd heard at night he screamed, "Look out!" Then he started laughing again.

Tony shook his head. "I think you're losing it, Tyler."

A nervous feeling swept through Sam as his eyes searched out ahead in the river once more. It was one thing to pray, but it was another thing not to know what was coming next. Then he remembered something his father had told him about things he couldn't see.

"That's what faith is," his father had said "You have to trust that God knows you, He sees you, and He hears you when you pray. You can't always see what's coming next in your life." Sam smiled. But his father had also told him, "You may not know what the future holds, so put your trust in the one who holds the future." They'd talked about that quite a bit after his father's heart attack scare.

A strange calm settled over Sam as those words drifted through his thoughts. For the first time he wasn't afraid. Even though he didn't know if they would make it out alive or not, strangely, he wasn't afraid anymore. But still he felt so small and the river looked so big…too big to survive, actually.

"Think I hear another one," Tony said.

All eyes turned toward the front of the raft. They scanned the river, looking for the next monster. Then everyone spotted it.

"Oh…my…goodness," Tyler shrieked. "That's worse than any so far."

"It *is* worse," Gus told them. "But it's not *the* worst. I'm telling you boys, we best get off this river somehow."

"But there's rocks the size of houses everywhere," Tyler cried.

"Hold on to that rudder," Sam ordered the others. "And steer us to the right as hard as you can."

The raft began easing in that direction until it hit another massive whirlpool. The force of those swirling waters turned the raft sideways just like before.

"Turn us around," Sam screamed. "There's another big one coming."

Tony, Tyler, and Gus strained against their makeshift rudder, but it was no use. The raft continued cascading down the river in a flurry of white water, rocks, spray, and thunder. Then they struck something so hard, all four rafters crashed onto the deck.

Sam raised his head up and noticed that, although the river continued its terrifying thunder, the raft was no longer moving. Now, only raging water rushed under them. He heard a sickening crack.

"We're breaking up," Tony shouted.

Sam pulled back the rubber pieces covering the raft. Water lashed against the logs. He also noticed that two of the heaviest raft logs were ready to split in half.

"We're tearing apart," he warned.

"Whadda we do now?" Tyler cried.

Just then they heard another noise, coming from somewhere no one could see. A rapid pop, pop, pop, cracked almost as loud as the roar of swirling waters crashing all around.

CHAPTER 17

IMPOSSIBLE RESCUE

Sam hurried to tie his safety rope to a tree branch sticking out between the rocks they had just hit. He looked around first to one side of the river and then the other, trying to find where that popping sound was coming from. Still he didn't see anything.

"Sounds like a speedboat or something," Tony shouted.

"Right," Tyler mocked. "Who'd be dumb enough to bring anything besides a rubber raft into these rapids?" Then he looked down at what was left of their wooden raft, and let out a nervous laugh. "Oh, never mind."

Next Sam looked up toward the sky and saw the most wonderful sight. Moving toward them was a rescue helicopter with a basket already hanging down. The main rotor chopped through the air with a pop, pop, pop.

"We're saved!" Tony hollered.

Tyler began jumping up and down on the raft and waving his

arms wildly. "Hey! We're down here. Help!"

"Stop jumping," Sam warned. "This whole thing could go to pieces any second."

"They already see us, Tyler," Tony said with a laugh. "What do you think that basket's for?"

Tyler began to tremble and sat down. "You mean…?" Tony nodded.

"Oh no you don't. I'm not riding up in any little basket on the end of some skinny rope."

"It's not a rope," Sam told him. "The cage is hooked to a metal cable. Probably strong enough to hold all of us if it had to."

"I don't care. You guys know how much I hate heights."

"Too late for that now," Sam said.

Tyler shook his head. "Oh no. Nothin' doin'."

"You got two choices," Tony told him. "You can ride up on the basket or float down to the category five rapids holding onto nothing but a stupid log."

Tyler trembled even more now. "I just don't know if I can make it."

"Sure you can," Sam told him. "It's your only chance."

"He's right," Gus said. He put a hand on Tyler's shoulder. "The river gets much worse up ahead. And even if you did make it through where we're stuck now, I doubt you'd survive the next stretch of rapids."

"It'd be like trying to go over Niagara Falls without a barrel," Tony said.

"Hey," Tyler said. "I heard of a guy who survived the falls and he went over with nothing but the clothes he was wearing and a smile."

Sam looked up again. "I'll bet he wasn't smiling." The helicopter stopped in the sky directly above them, and continued lowering the rescue basket. "Tyler. Here it comes. You first."

Tyler quickly backed away on the deck. Tony grabbed for him, but Tyler moved so far that if he'd gone another inch, he'd have been right back in the river. Tony crawled over and began dragging him forward. It took Sam, and Gus to help force Tyler into the basket. He kicked and screamed as they strapped him in. He never stopped screaming even after the men up in the helicopter had pulled him inside.

Tony went second. He climbed in the basket, pulled the straps tight, and it slowly rose, swaying gently from side to side in the air. He grabbed on tight to the basket and looked up at the powerful, churning blades of the main rotor.

Down below, the raft shifted in the water and nearly broke free from the rocks

Gus called out to Sam, "Why don't you go next? I'm old; I've had a full life."

"That's okay," Sam yelled back. He tightened his grip on the rope he'd tied to the branch. "You can go. I need to hold onto this rope or we might both drown."

"But I could trade spots with you."

Sam shook his head. "It's best this way."

When the basket came down again Gus reached up for it.

Then he turned to Sam. "You're a brave boy."

Sam smiled. "Get going. Will ya?"

Gus winked back at him and climbed into the basket. As he stepped off of the raft, it made another violent shift in the pounding current. With only Sam left on their raft now, the water under it began lifting the logs, threatening to blast them through the rocks and smash them into rapids below. Sam's eyes darted, looking for a big rock he could jump to in case the whole thing came apart and broke loose. Then he watched Gus climb inside the helicopter. Now the basket began descending to make its final rescue.

I hope it gets here in time, he thought. A log from the far side of the raft suddenly broke lose and water forced it underneath where Sam was standing. He felt it thump twice, then with a grinding, twisting sound, it spun around. The entire log went under water, but in seconds it shot back to the surface like an arrow from some giant's bow. Sam watched it sail through the air until it plunged deep into the water again. The massive log looked more like a matchstick, totally helpless against the river's furry.

When Sam glanced up again, the basket swung only a few feet from his grasp. He had to change his position and take a step closer, but when he did that, the raft shook and shifted, the logs groaned, and the whole thing began slowly turning around. In one last desperate move, Sam lunged for the basket, grabbing it with both hands. He dangled over the raging river while his rescue cage swung wildly from side to side after the helicopter dipped slightly. The raft below began breaking apart only inches from his feet. Sam felt sickness in his stomach along with relief in getting off that dangerous raft just in time.

While Sam struggled to pull himself up and into the basket, water splashed all over his face. As the helicopter's strong cable began pulling him higher, he could only stare down and watch in disbelief as the rest of the raft came completely apart, sending the logs, poles, food containers, sleeping bags, and everything else racing down the river. For an instant he imagined himself in the middle of all that fury. At that moment, his heart pounded, breathing quickened, yet he was thankful to be alive.

Just as his basket reached the side of the waiting helicopter, the crew grabbed it so Sam could climb in. When he was safe at last on the helicopter, Sam felt like crying…but he didn't. He was simply happy to have survived. He glanced over and saw Tyler wrapped in a blanket, huddled and shaking in a corner, far away from the open door.

A crew member, dressed in a flight suit and wearing a white helmet, gave each of them a headset. He motioned to put them on. Once they did that he said, "It's gonna be too loud, boys. With these on, you can talk to each other."

Sam turned and watched ahead, out the front windows. Their helicopter approached a wide spot beside the river a few miles from where the raft had become stranded. Tyler moved up and sat in a seat away from the open door. At first he refused to look out the window, but finally opened one eye and peeked. As they approached the wide beach, their helicopter stopped in mid-air for a few moments. The pilot called on the radio, "Rescue one on final approach, over."

Another voice crackled over the radio. "Roger. L Z cleared for landing."

Sam stared straight down. "Guys! Look at all those people down there. Are they waiting for *us*?" Tents, ATVs, four-wheel-drive trucks, and dozens of people milled around. When their helicopter began its descent, people below scattered like insects.

When they were only about a hundred feet from landing, Tyler said, "Hey Tony, isn't that your dad down there?"

Tony slid over to see where Tyler pointed. "Yeah. I think it is." Then he started waving out the window.

They touched down with a gentle thump and the blades spun to a stop. A rush of people quickly surrounded their helicopter and smiled when they saw the boys. Sam stumbled out first, then Tony and Tyler. Gus was the last one to be helped out, and a great roar went up from the crowd.

When they finally quieted down, Sam asked, "Do our parents know about us?"

Tony's father smiled. "The whole town's been praying for you boys back home."

Sam smiled. "Well, it worked."

"The rest of the parents are waiting in Moab."

"Mine too?" Tyler asked.

Mr. Dodds nodded.

His voice cracked. "*Both* of them?"

"Yes...both of them."

"Dad," Tony said. "This is our friend, Gus."

Tony's father put out his hand. "Nice to meet you, Gus."

"He's got a real..." Then he looked at Gus. "Is it okay to tell him?"

Gus nodded.

"A *real* gold mine, and we got to dig in it."

Just then a sheriff's officer walked over to where everyone was talking. "Anything I can do for you boys?"

"Yes," Sam said. "There are some men with motorcycles and guns. They tried to stop us." He turned and pointed to Gus. "He needs to get into Moab and file his claim. Right away."

"Come with me," the officer said. "You boys, too."

They all climbed back into the helicopter along with Tony's father. Tyler shuffled along behind the others and slowly climbed back in. He was still shaking from his first ride and his eyes had begun their famous Tyler twitching.

The pilot started the powerful, jet engine, and waited for the main rotor to come up to full speed. They gently lifted off from the beach, then went straight up into the air. The pilot sat there for less than a minute, and then the helicopter lurched forward. The nose dipped slightly, and the next thing Sam knew, they were flying like a bullet off toward Moab.

When they reached the town and landed at the sheriff's office, they found the rest of their families waiting there. After several hugs, kisses, and tears all around, Sam said, "Where's the place for Gus to file his claim?"

"Right here in the courthouse," an officer said. He motioned to them. "Follow me."

Sam walked next to the officer. "And Gus can tell you where it is. If your men go out there, you can still catch those guys."

"You don't think they'll be gone by now?"

"Some of them might, except a few should still be a little banged up."

"Banged up?"

Sam could hardly hold back his laugh. "We set some traps for them."

"But you said they had motorcycles."

"Had," Tony said with a big smile. "We did a little something to keep those from running, too."

"I'll send some of my men out there after Gus tells us where it is. Do you want to bring charges against them?"

"Gus nodded. I also want to fix it so the boys can be part owners in my gold mine."

"I'm sure that can be arranged."

Sam Tony and Tyler smiled at each other.

When Sam and his friends, along with Gus and the sheriff's officer, walked to the end of the hallway and turned the corner to go to the claims office, Sam's legs turned wobbly, his knees buckled, his head felt dizzy, and he almost dropped to the floor.

CHAPTER 18
GOLD MINE'S TRUE OWNER

Sam and his friends stopped dead still, right in the middle of the hallway. No one could believe who was sitting on a bench just outside the claims office.

Without moving his lips, Tony whispered. "Is that who I think it is?"

Sam gulped. "I'm sure of it."

"Is who, who?" Tyler asked.

"Don't you remember him?" Sam said. "He's the bald-headed guy who tried to grab our rope when we left."

Tyler could barely squeak. "He is?"

"How could you forget?" Tony asked.

When the scary man saw them, he quickly looked away, pretending he hadn't noticed.

Sam turned to Gus. "He's trying to steal your gold, just like you said."

"You know that man?" the officer asked.

Sam nodded.

"What are we gonna do?" Tony asked.

Sam motioned for everyone to follow. "Come on." He and the others began walking again.

When they reached the door to the claims office, Sam saw a note that said, "Back in fifteen minutes."

"Whew," he sighed, "that's a break."

About a minute later, a man wearing a suit came walking down the hallway toward the office. A ring of keys jingled in his hand with each step he took.

"There he is now," the sheriff's deputy said.

"But..." Tony said. He looked at the biker, dressed in black leather, sitting on a bench on the other side of the hallway.

Tyler ducked down, "Who?"

The big man Tony had been looking at stood. He looked even bigger, close up, than he did when they had seen him out by the gold mine. *How did he get here before we did?* Sam wondered. The man's face and hands were scraped and cut.

"My, my, my," the man with the keys said as he turned the lock on his office door. "I might not see so many people in a month. What's all this about?"

The large man and Gus said at the same time, "I'm here to file my claim." Then they turned and glared at each other.

"You both have the same claim or two different ones?"

"Same," Gus said.

"Different," the big man said through gritted teeth.

The officer rubbed the sides of his chin. “This *is* confusing.”

With all the courage he could find, Sam stepped in front of the big man, blocking his path into the claims office. “Officer,” he said to the policeman, “arrest this man.”

“On what grounds?”

“We have all kinds of reasons,” Tony said.

“Yeah,” Tyler’s weak voice added.

The biker pushed his way into the room and stood at the counter next to Gus who wasn’t half his size.

“You have to show me some gold, first,” the claims office clerk said.

The big man flashed an evil smile, opened his mouth, and pointed at his gold fillings.

“From your mine,” the clerk told him.

Sam gulped. Tyler’s voice quivered even more now. He pulled out both of his empty pockets. “We lost ours on the raft.”

“Who says the gold in my mouth didn’t come from my own mine?” the big man demanded.

“That’s a good point.” He turned to the sheriff’s officer. “What do you say?”

“I think this is one for the judge to decide.”

“This is just like when King Solomon was about to divide that baby in half,” Tyler sighed.

Gus looked around the room filled with people, cleared his throat, reached into his shirt, and pulled out a small, leather pouch tied around his neck. “I think this is what you’re looking for,” he said with a broad grin. Then he loosened the top, pulled open the pouch, and poured some of the most beautiful gold nuggets anyone could imagine onto a hard, shiny countertop. The nuggets sounded like pebbles as they hit the counter. Gus handed two of the biggest gold nuggets to the man behind the counter, and flashed a broad big smile. "Will these do?"

The clerk stared down at the gold, looked back up to Gus and said, "Well, sir. I'll just have to go into the back room and run a little test."

When the clerk turned to leave, the biker grabbed as many of the nuggets as he could from the counter, and bolted for the door. The sheriff's officer, and all three boys, grabbed him and wrestled the man to the floor. Even Gus piled on top.

The police officer called for help on his radio and soon several other deputies stormed into the room to help handcuff and arrest the big man.

An officer held the prisoner by one arm. "Good thing our jail is right in this building. Got a nice cell just waiting for you."

The sheriff gave the order, and soon his officers hurried out to Gus' claim where they arrested all of the other gang members.

"Be careful on the path," Sam warned. "We set a lot of traps out there."

"Thanks," one of the officers said. "We'll watch out for them."

The next day, after all the paperwork was finished, Sam, Tony, and Tyler were invited back out to Gus' cabin. Their fathers came too. Sam and Tony walked out ahead of the group so they could undo the remaining fish line traps. With shovels, they filled the holes in the path, and pulled the rest of the sharp sticks that were still poking out of the ground.

"You guys set all of these?" Sam's father asked.

Sam smiled at him and nodded.

His father nodded back. "Pretty smart."

Just then, Tony's foot kicked into the last trip wire, releasing a strong branch that caught him right in the chest, just like before, and threw him off the path.

His father rushed to help him up. "You okay, buddy?"

Tony dusted himself off and said, "It'd take more than a tree branch to hurt me."

"This is why we wanted to walk ahead of the rest of you," Sam said. "It's what we were doing while Tyler and Gus worked in the mine that night."

"Yeah," Tony said as he walked back on the path. "And Sam put sugar in the bikers' gas tanks, too." He started laughing, "Man, you shoulda seen those guys when their big bikes stopped running. It was like a guy with a gun and no bullets."

After all the traps had been removed, everyone walked down to Gus' campsite. Sam and his friends were able to show them where the secret mine was; a mine that they now partly owned.

"You boys are welcome to come out here any summer you want and help me work this place," Gus told them with a smile. "And the gold I find the rest of the year belongs to the four of us."

"Really?" Tyler squeaked.

The old man nodded with a smile. He looked to Sam. "You

boys saved the mine, and you saved my life." He turned to Sam's friends. "We're partners, four ways."

Sam didn't want to leave, but he knew it was time to head home. He also knew he would never forget what had happened. God helped him when he prayed, and he'd never forget about Gus.

As they were about ready to leave the mine, everyone heard a sound. "There's that bell again," Tony said.

"Lucky?" Tyler shouted. He ran toward the direction of the sound.

Because of what happened to the boys' raft, Tony's uncle had to find another job, but he didn't mind. "I was getting a little tired of going down the same old river, over and over, day after day anyway," he told them.

"And you boys are gonna have to stop getting into so much trouble," Tony's father said.

"Right," Sam's dad added.

"Tyler, I've done some serious thinking about you and my family," his father told him.

Tyler looked up at him and smiled.

That's something Sam had hoped to hear ever since Tyler first talked about his family's troubles.

"All right, everyone," Sam's father said. "Time to head out. I know three moms who can't wait to get you back."

Even though it was still several weeks away, Sam could hardly wait to get to school. This was one year when he would have a story to tell his new friends that was just as exciting as the one Tony had.

That made Sam Cooper grin. *With everything that's already happened this summer, we couldn't possibly get into any more trouble...could we?*

- THE END -

ABOUT THE AUTHOR

Max Elliot Anderson grew up as a reluctant reader. After surveying the market, he sensed the need for action-adventures and mysteries for readers eight and up, especially boys.

Mr. Anderson was a producer of the nationally televised PBS special, *Gospel at the Symphony,* that was nominated for an Emmy, and won a Grammy for the double album soundtrack. He won a best cinematographer award for the film, *Pilgrim's Progress*, which was the first feature film in which Liam Neeson had a starring role. He has produced, directed, or shot over 500 national television commercials for True Value Hardware Stores.

Mr. Anderson owns *The Market Place*, a client-based video production company for medical and industrial clients. His productions have taken him all over the world including India, New Guinea, Europe, Canada, and across the United States.

Using his extensive experience in the production of motion pictures, videos, and television commercials, Mr. Anderson brings the same visual excitement and heart-pounding action to his stories. With the exception of the Sam Cooper Adventures, each book has completely different characters, setting, and plot.

Young readers have reported that reading one of Mr. Anderson's books is like being in an exciting or scary movie.

Author Web Site:

http://www.maxbooks.9k.com/index_1.html

Books for Boys Blog: booksandboys.blogspot.com/

Mr. Anderson is listed in WHO'S WHO in Finance and Industry, Entertainment, Advertising, The Midwest, Emerging Leaders in America, The World, and WHO'S WHO In America (1999 - present)

CPSIA information can be obtained at www.ICGtesting.com
Printed in the USA
BVOW02s2015190813

328662BV00005B/274/P